BETWEEN TIDES

BETWEEN TIDES

— A NOVEL —

ANGEL KHOURY

DZANC
BOOKS

2580 Craig Rd.
Ann Arbor, MI 48103
www.dzancbooks.org

Library of Congress Cataloging-in-Publication Data Available Upon Request

ISBN: 978-1-950539-32-1
First US edition: August 2021
Interior design by Michelle Dotter
Cover by Matthew Revert

Printed in the United States of America

10   9   8   7   6   5   4   3   2   1

for
LCE and DCF
and forever and always
NGM

"Go, go, go, said the bird: human kind
Cannot bear very much reality."

—T. S. Eliot

PROLOGUE

Perhaps I am obsessed.
I answer, and so?
If the tide were always in, or always out,
if there were no space, however infinitesimal, between tides,
where fractional change occurs,
where nothing, something, everything is or isn't,
there would be no place for desire.
It is the unbridgeable space between two fleshly beings
that enlivens me, that haunts me,
the close chasm between reach and grasp.
And if that boundary exists in the flesh,
why can it not live on between the mortal and the dead?
If it is the unbridgeable that binds us,
does it matter from which side of earth
we reach for one another?

ONE

I THOUGHT I HEARD A BABY CRYING. Perhaps it was the wind. No, for as I make my way from parlor to vestibule, I see a vague shape in the watery light. Slender as a blue heron, it dips and preens. Something, someone, stands there knocking.

A young woman is turning, about to leave. Not a baby then. Not a bird. Still, something familiar, embedded in memory, like the faint profile couched in the downy folds of a pillow, still smelling of depthless sleep or vivid dream.

— Gillian. With a hard *G*, Gillian Lodge, she says. She extends one long-fingered hand, keeping the other clamped to her side.

— And Lodge? Is that with a soft *G*? I start to ask.

I gather my manners. I well know how to pronounce our shared last name.

— I'm here to learn something of my father's life up here at Cape Cod, she says. Gilead? Gilead Lodge?

That Carolina drawl.

I should shut the door. But no. I stand back just far enough to stare up and down the length of her.

This child of my belated husband is too young to be my daughter, if I'd had one, too young even for a granddaughter, for I am of an age when, by rights, I should have great-grandchildren gathered at my knee.

I invite Gil's daughter in. How could I not? I move stacks of *The Auk* and Grinnell's *Forest and Stream* to make a place for her. Somehow without my noticing, uneven piles of magazines ring the room, high as the back of the settee, so that the parlor seems a feathered nest.

In her navy Red Cross uniform, this Gillian Lodge could be my own Gil, except that his Life-Saving Service uniform was a faded cornflower blue, scrubbed soft by my hands and neatly pressed for as long as the wind off Chatham Bar would allow. Her uniform is so new, it's as though the cloth's been pulled straight off the bolt and pinned to her slim frame. She is tall, like him, with a way of looking out of her eyes as though from a body only borrowed.

I look more closely, and now I see her mother's favor, the widow's peak, the tiny mole at the corner of her mouth. It spoils her for me, breaks the spell. She's no more like him than a bird in molt, standing drab before me, while his memory looms brilliant in my mind.

I wonder how she sees me, and not just me, but how I surround myself, here in a house once white as a wedding cake, elaborate with frosting. The last of the paint peeled long ago from its ornamented stickwork and gabled eaves. The year the weather finally planed its boards back down to raw wood was the year I gathered myself into its core, shutters latched.

TWO

GILLIAN SITS WITH MY DOG AT HER FEET. She is young, does not know, has no history of me, or perhaps even of him, her father old and dead by the time she was scarcely taller than his knee. She seems puzzled that I would have a Chesapeake named Dash, the same as her retriever back home. I've lost count of my dogs descended from her father's Dash, enough to fill three duck boats. Likely another three boatloads' worth of Dashes have been born in Carolina. Even his dog, I have had to share.

— Why does my Chessie surprise you? Didn't anyone tell you he and I had a dog named Dash?

— You're my father's sister?

— You said you wanted to know about your father. I don't know why you didn't ask your mother, but then, what has that woman ever understood of our mutual husband.

— What did you say?

She pulls her hand away from Dash's head.

— Didn't they tell you he left me both husbandless and dogless so that I, too proud to beg him to stay, was left to beg one of Dash's puppies? Have you the least idea what that was like?

Dash whines deep in his throat. She stands.

— I need to leave.

This daughter will someday tell how I stood back and glared. Why have you come back to haunt me after all these years? she will claim I said. Then comes the slamming of the door, and the desperate run all the way down to the end of Main, to the Hotel Mattaquason, and up to her room, crying.

She will refuse supper: oyster stew or lobster bisque, this detail changing, why? Maybe it's what she's hungry for on any given day, ten or twenty years from now. She will remember the room number, how at first she did not hear the knock. Then her mind will wander and, as she will tell it, someone will give one sharp rap, or perhaps three hard slaps of an open palm, jiggle the knob, and say to her through the locked door, you are family, you must come home with me. She will wish it true, but it will not be me, Blythe Harding Lodge, who invites her home.

No, she is not mine, this one who takes the truth and tosses it up to see how it will land. In this, she is her mother's daughter, too overwrought for my liking, and yet somehow, she captivates.

This one could be mine.

THREE

It's fortunate I'm an early riser. She's at my door before the coffee's finished brewing.

— It's me, Gillian, she says.

I don't correct her grammar. Nor do I remind her that we met just yesterday, and my memory is fine. Why bother. Next thing, she'll be telling me it's 1942, and there's a war on.

— Gilly. That's what your father called you. It will do for me.

I don't say, what kind of made-up name is Gillian.

I see her gaze skipping, like a bit of shell just so across the water, over the few toys scattered about, the well-thumbed books of fairy tales, the children's pictures sketched in wax or chalk that show the true scale of things: whales and people, hermit-crab shells and houses, all of a size, equal in importance. I know what will catch her eye.

Ah, good for her; she seems unfazed. The stuffed shorebirds and the songbirds and the birds of prey, the swan whose wingspan is wider than the French doors, the gaudy puffin and the demure sandpiper, she studies each, but only for a moment. She shows no favorites, committing to none. I am now the curator of my own private natural history museum, where the public is never invited. And yet, I've let her in.

Gilly untucks her hands and they move restlessly from waist to lap to head. When she tugs at the dark hair at the back of her neck with her fingers clutched and then spread, I have to look away.

She walks to the window, or as close as she can get.

— Wouldn't you like me to open these? she asks.

The brocade draperies no longer reach the floor. I've taken the scissors to them any number of times, after one dog or another has cocked his leg. What's left of the threadbare fabric, once richly figured in reds and golds, no longer recalls its intended pattern, but shuttles new designs, the sun weaving them yellow, the moon stitching them white. I can spend minutes or hours, hands held out as though to the heat of a flame, aligning the light that filters through the brocade's dappled rot with my own tracery of skin.

— No.

She sits down.

I offer her a cognac but she prefers coffee. She holds her cup in two hands, except for those occasional disquieting tugs.

— Never turn down a good scotch whiskey or a cognac, I tell her.

At least she takes her coffee black.

— So, what do you want to know? I ask.

She launches right in, words spilling over each other.

— Slow down, I say.

I have a hard time understanding her, with her one-syllable words pulled like salt taffy into three. It calls to mind those Hatterasmen who hauled me out of the mailboat the day I arrived looking for her father.

— Yes, even the students at college couldn't understand me, she says. Even if they were all from North Carolina. Professor Rose always did say there's the State of North Carolina, and then there's the State of Dare. Our county's so far out to sea, you'd be just as likely to wash ashore as to actively want to get there. Neither happens much. Just enough to make things interesting.

A college girl. Gil would have been pleased with her ambition, as well as this apt characterization of the place of her birth, to which I can certainly attest.

— You, I could listen to you speak all day, she says. Your accent reminds me so much of my father.

— My husband.

She doesn't flinch. Still, I can feel her eyes on me. She asks all around the subject, his parents, his childhood, skipping over the part about him, about him and me. I don't answer. Now that I have her here, I intend to do the asking.

— All right, then. Do you want to know about your father?

I start to stand, then think better of it. I want to be at eye level with her. But she looks down, fiddling with Dash's rough curls, so I speak to the top of her head, to the cowlick I expect to find, and do. Saying:

— *The first time Gil went to Carolina was in 1866. He left in the boat he had built himself and christened with a bottle of whiskey instead of champagne. That trip wasn't an escape from something, more a flight to something, to the place where his brother, Ben, had died.*

Gil's daughter fidgets in her chair. My trance breaks. This is why I don't bother with people. They can't begin to see where fractional change occurs, where nothing, something, everything is or isn't.

FOUR

— I KNOW ABOUT HIM, MY FATHER'S BROTHER, she says. I heard how Papa came looking for Uncle Benjamin. Wasn't anything left in the marsh to find of him, or a lot of other Yankees who made the mistake of coming south.

And this one wants to go off to this latest conflagration, a World War, capital Ws, with a Roman Numeral Two behind it? She bears her father's hubris like the self-same arch of their brows. I ignore her and go on:

— *If a boat is the sum total of the man who built it, then stem to stern, his whiskey-drenched sharpie, every inch of it, was Gil, all except the name he gave it, N-Seine, though there would be some to dispute it.*

She interrupts. Again. Looking straight at me, she says she hasn't much time. She's leaving for England soon. She's come to learn about her father's life here, *here*, she repeats, and she has a list, she says.

A list.

She pulls something from her pocket and unfolds it. My eyesight is good. I can see even from here she's typed a full page, no less, with numbers running down the length of it.

— Let's cut the questions into strips, I say. We'll put them in Dash's bowl and mix them around. We'll have a drawing. I'll even let you choose. I will answer one, and only one, of your questions.

She looks startled, and then, thinking I'm teasing, she laughs.

— Let me see it, I say.

She hands me the page. No, there are two. I look them over, and then tear them, not into neatly framed questions, but into indecipherable mutterings that clamor on the floor at my feet.

— What you think you want to know and what you need to know are two different things.

Maybe she'll leave.

She smiles in a way that is painful to see, his smile, his lips, those teeth. Leaning over, she pets Dash, threads his tail through her hand.

— So, there was another Dash somewhere back in time? Kin both to you and to my own sweet boy?

The traitor, he puts his paws on her shoulders and gives her a lick.

— Come back tomorrow, I tell Gil's youngest.

She flashes the smile that catches at her teeth and is out of the house and down the lane before I can rise from my chair. I wonder how it's possible to inherit something such as forgetting to shut the door.

FIVE

WHAT SHALL I TELL HER? Shall I say how at night or on blow days too windy to hunt, her father would sit at his workbench, a six-foot bird of prey hulking over its kill—how he would sit immobile, the hourglass leaking time, as he dissected a tiny shorebird that, bones and all, barely weighed two ounces? How he would spend hours picking the bird to pieces, then breathe its soul into a new body of his own making?

Surely I will not tell how, more than his hands, I liked to watch his mind work over the bird, his careful measurements extrapolated into precise communion, arranging the sanderling in arrested flight, the sum total of its essence expressed in a wingbeat stilled, that said: This, this is what it means to be a sanderling! If he happened to glance up, he would look out of startled eyes as though he'd crawled into the skin of a bird, was looking out through its bright bead, was become bird, more than bird, was flight.

What I will not tell her, or perhaps I do, is how I imagined him arranging my limbs as he did the sanderling's wings, smoothing them down or flaring them out, standing back to see what pleased him best. How would I look, who would I be, molded by hands that lingered, fingers finding hollows and swells? I held my breath, caught between heartbeats, as though I were a bird caged, peering out through his ribs.

Say I told her these things, or perhaps she made them up. But then, what does it matter. Reality, I think, is mostly imagination, poorly disguised.

SIX

MISS GILLY LODGE HAS RETURNED. She stands just inside the door, the ruby-stained glass on the portside of the entry hall spangling her face. She steals glances, not shy, but like a child who thinks if she doesn't look at you, you can't see her. Then again, who could be at ease, knocking on my door after all these years?

— I'm here a few more days, she says. You may as well go ahead and tell me more.

She comes, wanting answers, polite, then demanding, what to make of this man she barely remembers. Like me, so naïve to think she could come at him unawares.

Another blink of these old eyes and he's back in my doorway, back in Chatham, on our own Cape Cod. Yet I well know he lies on a faraway island, six feet down, beneath a tombstone carrying the weighty lineage of all who have come before him, the last man to bear the name Lodge.

Why should she come to disturb my final days, now when my time is waning?

She carries our cups to the side porch looking out toward Nauset Beach. It's a fine day, dew on the roses. I see the view through her eyes, approving. But how, I wonder, does she see me? She might see a cumulus of hair, drifted by the least wind, in which she could claim shapes: a teacup, or daffodils, a volcano erupted, or, if she's lacking in imagination, simply a full head of hair in need of a trim.

She cannot know, and her father would not have told her, that this hair was once yellow. He would not have told her how he spread it in a fan, just at the edge of the sea, where the waves pack the sand smooth, how he would gem the swirled strands, studding them with yellow coquinas, lavender periwinkles, with a razor clam for a bar-rette, and then laugh as a wave slapped my cheek and swept them all away.

If she would lift her pretty head to focus on my face instead of her feet, she would think my eyes merely brown. They were once, by his lights, the color of honeycomb, containing all colors, as bees fly sticky laden with the color of all flowers.

No, she sees me, a cloudy-headed thing, and thinks, *Old*.

Her father said these things, or I expect he might have, if he could have put looks into words. Perhaps he did say them. It's been so very long.

Here she comes now, to make those days flare up again, bright as the sun. And I, an old woman, a dying ember soon to be ash, reach for them gladly.

— Are you ready? I ask. All right, then. And don't interrupt.

I look out across the rugosa roses to the blue harbor, the yellow strand, the ocean just beyond. No need of sight. No need to gather my thoughts. I begin.

SEVEN

As everyone knows by now, that first trip to Carolina didn't fix whatever some people thought was wrong with Gilead Lodge. It was his first trip, but not his last, and I'll never know whether it was his first or his fifth journey to Cape Hatteras that finally spelled the end of our marriage.

The War of the Rebellion was one year past. Gil was sixteen, nearly seventeen, his brother, Ben, dead for five long years. By then, my own mourning was done. Life in our town of Chatham, on the spurred heel of the Cape, kept its own pace. Schooners docking or wrecking on the shoals or passing us by, cranberry bogs sanded and flooded and swarmed over by a thousand pickers laughing and singing and gossiping as they moved through a crimson tide. The cloth sails of the saltwork mills cartwheeled, as ever, against the sky, the spring run of cod giving every boy in town an excuse to miss school. Our boys in blue had come home, or not. The war was ended.

In a way, I was glad no one seemed to recall how Ben would walk me home from church or come by my house with a book to loan or, shyly, to give, not waiting for me to read his inscription. I had adjusted. At twenty-four, I already considered myself an old maid. Everyone was worried about Gil.

It was as if the day Gil learned of his brother's death played over and over in his mind, the milk pooling on the mahogany table, soaking the torn edge of the envelope, then dripping onto the Turkey carpet. He saw himself pummeling through the gate that always clipped his ankle, the gate Ben was forever telling him not to slam. Saw himself running down the dust-drenched street, to the landing where his dory was tied, an easy vault over the piling and into the boat, the slipknot unraveling in his hand that still clenched the envelope already souring in the heat of his palm. Watched the knot come undone with one simple tug, just as Ben had made him practice till he'd gotten it right, saw fluttering from his other fist shredded bits of telegram sending their hyphenated news, a syllable here, a word there, and the envelope's dreaded star signifying death, swirling around inside the boat's hull, washing back and forth in the bilge water. The dory rocked with the solid weight of a twelve-year-old boy, then stilled. After that, only erratic shudders, port and starboard, sending ripples like dots and dashes out across the bay.

EIGHT

I'D NEVER PAID MUCH ATTENTION TO GIL, eight years younger than Ben and me. My first sturdy memory of him was the day of Ben's service. It was an Indian summer day bright under a high blue dome but with whitecaps piled on the horizon. The *Chatham Monitor* had run the notice in the previous Tuesday's edition, calling it a funeral, but it was an empty ritual, no body to bury, just a tombstone rising above a boneless grave.

Gil stood off to himself, holding a kingfisher's feather in both hands. It made me recall Ben's fondness for the bird. A halcyon, he had called it, a fabled bird the Greeks believed could calm the wind and waves. This boy knows his brother well, I thought, how sweet, expecting him to place the blue-gray feather in amongst the lilies overflowing the marble urn.

Before the minister could conclude a service that would discreetly omit the familiar "earth to earth, ashes to ashes, dust to dust," the boy had thrown the feather to the ground. It fluttered as though about to take wing, but then settled onto the sod unturned and all green underfoot, no need for gravediggers. He ran zigzagging between the lichened stones, set in place so long ago that their names and dates were inscribed twice, first by the stonecutter and then written again in mossy script. They leaned or sighed into the earth—all except Ben's upright marker, an affront to the entire congregation of stones, his name a raw scar chiseling hard fact:

BENJAMIN CHARLES LODGE
Captain, US Navy
b. June 27, 1841
Chatham, Mass.
d. Oct. 4, 1861
Chicamacomico, NC

I followed Ben's little brother through the cemetery gates and down the street. Gil would later tell the story, my head in his lap, twisting my hair in his fingers: how he sat there crouched in the baker's alley and watched me run past. How he was not surprised when I turned back into the alley and picked him up, his tall frame gone bony in a spurt of growth. How, enfolded in the moiré skirts of my gown, he reeled away from the smell of beach plum and rugosa and cranberries, fruity, salt-tanged, and tart, as shocked as if Ben himself had scooped him up from the rancid stones.

On Ben's dresser, Gil later told me, was a small whalebone box scrimshawed with two hearts entwined, our initials centered in each. Inside, pungent as the day Ben shipped out, was a scattering of desiccated leaves, air-brittled petals, and shriveled berries still red. Gil would recall how the alley, yeasty and sour, receded, overtaken by the scent of beach and bluff and bog, the smells he had breathed each night before bedtime, thinking, *Ben.*

Neither of us remembered, but there are those who do (the first of many claiming prescience), that two boys ran into the alley, kicking a can along the cobblestones. They saw a tall, fair-haired woman in black standing next to the rain barrel, clasping a boy in Sunday clothes. It was a school day, and what had begun as tardiness was now outright truancy, recess nearly over. They could hear from two blocks away each shriek and whoop and belly laugh in the schoolyard, single notes making up the song of an ordinary day. If one could only choose such a happy refrain instead of that chorus of unending loss.

NINE

THERE WAS A TIME, quite a long period of time it seems, when my life appeared to flow like the bankless blue river of the Gulf Stream, at times narrow or broad, but always of a piece.

Now, a decade ago sounds as likely as a week gone past. I seem to have arrived at a place of slippage. Upheaval. Disjointedness. Years go by very fast. Minutes pass very slowly. In between is a bent place, where the outward and the inward only occasionally converge. And so I sit here vigilant, attending to the effort of remaining faithful to the moment.

Gilly is here to learn about her father, so why does my mind veer back, where it never goes, back to that time before Gil? I lost interest long ago, so why should I flatter myself that Gilly would be interested in my own life, would wonder about my upbringing, my family, me.

It was just as well she never asked. My family was no more relevant to my daily life than an understudy in the wings to an audience held spellbound by players declaiming from center stage.

My mother lived her life with one foot in heaven and one foot in hell. My father spent his life trying to keep her from rending herself in two. Neither, therefore, had the strength to attend to anyone else who might stand on the brink of her own daily precipice. Her demons pocketed the keys to our house. They left the door wide open for me to do as I pleased.

I went away to school, made a few acquaintances, corresponded with them until one or the other of us stopped writing. I never seemed to have an aptitude for friendship, and truth be told, never wished it otherwise.

Now that I've surpassed twice my mother's age, I can wonder at the state of our upbringing. My sister married a sailmaker from Harwich whose most reliable address was an India-bound clipper. She died in childbirth the same week he died of ship fever. She was buried in Seaside Cemetery, spared the knowledge that her husband's plot was fathoms deep, that he was tilted overboard in a hard wind that blew him sideways off the plank, tied up in a canvas shroud bearing his own stitch marks. Their orphaned son was taken away by his family in Maine. Ezekiel Lawrence was his name. For a time, I called him Ezra. Ezra Lodge.

TEN

PEOPLE LIKE TO TALK ABOUT THE MAN WITH TWO WIVES, but I rather like to think about two wives with no husband. For Gil was wed not to us, but to a place, and to that place he was the most faithful of men. He never cheated on his two beloveds, Hatteras and Bodie islands. It was there, at one or the other of those desolate places, that he slept most nights, laid out long with an arm outstretched on humid summer evenings, or curled in close against a cold northeaster, alone.

He told each of us he wanted to live at Cape Hatteras. I said no, never would I leave the Cape, as for me, there is only one cape, my own. She, born out of those Hatteras sands, said no, never would she continue to live there, not once she had become addicted to that whiff of *away* that clung to him. She made it a condition of their marriage that he would take her from Hatteras. The farthest she got was Roanoke, one island from home, not even half a day's sail on a decent wind.

— You do realize I know your mother, don't you? I ask Gilly.

— What? You do? She never told me. How can that be?

She draws her knees up under her chin and curls her bare toes. Thankfully, she's no longer wearing that stiff uniform and is instead dressed like someone who knows how to live here—clothes a second skin, not an adornment. She sits on her feet, frowning.

— I once caught Papa looking at a miniature. He put it away when I came in. I knew how to pull up the side panel in his lap desk to unlatch the secret compartment under the sand well. Later, I took a peek at it.

She looks me over. Stands up, crosses the room, puts her finger under my chin, the impertinent thing, and turns my head in profile.

— I see. Oh Mrs. Lodge—no, that sounds funny, you look nothing like my mother, I mean she's Mrs. Lodge, can I call you Blythe? Oh Blythe, I think it must have been you. In the portrait.

I'm surprised. I didn't know there was a miniature of me, much less that it lived in Carolina, in a hidden compartment. But still. He had me there. With him.

I move away, into the kitchen, look up at the top pantry shelf so that the tears will roll into my hairline like the marsh soaking up the tide.

— Dash! Supper!

Gilly follows me, absentmindedly takes the cup of food from my hand and pours it into his bowl.

— Well, anyway, she says, one night I was hiding behind the settee when Papa came in from Bodie Island. He still had on his waders. That's all I could see, his rubber soles, until I crawled to the corner for a better view. He went straight to his lap desk, opened the secret compartment, and held the portrait in one hand, tugging his hair with the other like he did when he had something on his mind, so I knew to be still. I was glad I was, because Mother came in. I couldn't see her face but I could see his. He had that same look like when I got found out, stealing a drumstick to go crabbing when a chicken neck would have done just fine.

While Gilly fills Dash's water bowl, I busy myself rearranging the silverware in the drawer, as if I care which spoons go where or whether they need polishing. I know that look of Gil's, mostly by its absence. It was that rare to see in him any evidence of self-reflection—not in his nature, no more than an osprey would wonder why it had caught this sea mullet, not that one.

— The next time I went to look at the miniature, Gilly says, the little wooden divider was broken. I pushed on the false bottom of the sand well. The secret compartment was empty. Well actually, it wasn't empty. The portrait was gone. But there were ashes in the little niche. Later when I was in bed, I heard Mother shout, *There is no such person! She doesn't exist!* I thought she was talking about a ghost and started crying. She came into my room and said to hush. I guess in her mind, you don't. Exist, I mean. Or else why didn't she tell me about you before I came all this way. Here I land on your doorstep, thinking from what the storekeeper at the Mayflower said, you weren't, well, my stepmother, you were just someone who used to know my father.

Gilly sees my look. The one that says I am not your stepmother. Don't presume. She flushes.

— That was cruel of my mother, my sisters too. To let me come up here, not even knowing my father had a wife, well I mean, you know, another wife, to let me just come here bumbling around like an idiot.

I take pity and don't agree that she was a bumbling idiot. I blame the mother. But then, I always did.

— And now you're telling me not only did my mother see you in the portrait, but she's met you?

— Oh, yes, on my one and only trip south, in the winter of '93, the second time Gil went away. After he had deserted his position at the life-saving station, left his hotel business, his home, me. After I'd found out he was living on Hatteras Island, using a different name, I'd gone to Carolina to bring him back home.

— A different name? That seems a bit dramatic. He really didn't want you to, I mean, he really didn't want to be found.

My look serves its purpose. She changes the subject.

— What did you think of my mother? Gilly asks.

— Shall I tell you? I suppose I should.

When I first saw Maud O'Neal, she was sitting like an angel in the precise center of a cloud, black hair falling past her waist to disappear in drifting billows of down. A half-dozen whistling swans, long necks dangling, hung from the porch eave, while plucked birds lay like pale shadows beneath them, their pimpled flesh recoiling from the splintered floorboards. Gil's gun, and her dog, leaned at ease against his thigh.

When the girl sneezes, Gil laughs and reaches for a white feather as it drifts past. He holds it under her chin like a buttercup, and predicts future happiness, and it will seem so. For the human capacity to make wishful thinking true is a powerful one, and this girl will forever see lightning bolts where there are only fireflies.

ELEVEN

IF IT WEREN'T THE MINIATURE, it would be something else, Gilly says. Although actually she was glad when her parents argued because Gil would take her away with him, for a day or a week at a time. She was selfish with him that way.

Selfish with words, as well, it seems. So I must do the work for her, make sense of her disjointed thoughts—sea oats, mountains, screenwire, drawers—and so Gilly says, or might have said, how:

Gilly and her papa met the Trenton on the Manteo wharf. She remembers how Captain Johnson heaved the sacks of burlap filled with seeds over the rail and down into Papa's shadboat, how the bags got tall, the boat got low, how Papa lifted her down among the sacks and she scrambled over the rough, shifting bags to reach down into the water, how she imagined, looking at her reflection, that she was not on a boat, but up on a mountain, with the brown sacks ranging high all around her, the sea oats shifting inside.

She sticks her leg in the crevice between two sacks, swallowed by an earthquake, or almost.

— Running mighty low in the water there, Cap'n Lodge, says Captain Johnson.

— Tide's lifting. She'll be fine.

— Going to farming, are ye?

— You might say.

Gilly believes her father saves up his words with other people so he can spend them all on her. He is surely a millionaire, then, and she a great heiress someday.

She can tell by the way he stretches his legs out in the boat that today he'll spend some of his fortune on her.

— You ready to plant these sea oats alongside where you helped me to put the pine saplings? he asks.

The white sail unfolds itself into a triangle. He elbows the tiller, and the boat, despite the extra weight, springs out of Doughs Creek and into Shallowbag Bay. She stands at the prow and points south, wordlessly commanding his compass point. Her mother says she babbles, but she can save up words as well as anyone.

— I had them shipped here from Cape Cod, he says.

Another reason to hold her tongue. Those two words are almost never spoken by her father. When her mother speaks them, he will leave and be gone for days. Still, his legs remain outstretched, and they are on the water, so all is well.

— Since we last cut the pine saplings and staked them in rows, the needles have caught the sand, he tells her. We've grown ourselves a sand dune and now we're ready to plant it with sea oats to keep the dune in place, keep it high enough to break the wind.

— Once upon a time, the people cut down the trees and turned them into ships that rode upon the wind, and the wind blew the ships and the sand and the geese, she says.

— And?

— And we're using this sand to outsmart the other sand so it will stay out of the ponds for the geese so you can shoot them and then they will sail on the ships to market.

— I'm out of that now. No more market hunting.

He draws his legs in. The words slow to a trickle.

— Come back astern with me. We're about to leave the bay.

She isn't afraid of the waves or the boat riding so low. People say he's the best on the water they've ever seen, Yankee or no.

— Is it time for geography? she asks, leaning against him.

— All right. Pay attention. Tonight we'll draw a map.

— Coming up on John's Ditch, she says, standing up on the juniper thwart, her elbow propped on his shoulder.

She correctly calls out the moves through the narrow creek, hard to starboard, then port, port! Straight up the middle, and on, together they read the subtleties of black needlerush and mudflats that all look the same, unless you know the signposts: a clump of lavender marsh mallows, a path the width of deer walking single file, a cedar blasted by lightning looking for a place to go to ground, the kingfisher sitting year after year on the same rotted hull, surveying his domain.

— Due south, coming up on Maggie's Drawers, she calls out. Hard to portside, turn, turn!

Her two small hands not even covering his one on the tiller, she stands braced against him. Here is the part she likes the least, when he hauls in the mainsail and steps astern to jolt the naphtha engine to life. No longer silently skating across the water, they sputter into the narrow slit through the marsh, where the air is close, rank, and fecund with the smell of fish larvae and a thousand million shrimp gestating in the estuary's tide-swollen belly.

TWELVE

— *Tight as Maggie's Drawers through there, the men would say* of an afternoon, working over a length of net.

They talk over the child as though she were an egret hearing minnow's words, not men's, and she, like an egret poised to spear the meaning of a word, whispering it to herself, holds it in her throat for a while, trying to digest it.

— Not so tight anymore, I heard tell.

— No way she's taken up with Screenwire, even if he didn't have no wife ever since this time last week. Deader 'n a day-old croaker, she keeled over picking collards, they said, and he didn't notice her laying there right off, which pretty much sums up her looks.

— You've gone and done it now, saying his old lady was big-headed and wrinkled up as an old collard leaf.

—You said it, not me. All's I said was he never noticed her laying there, not till he come in for supper and weren't nothing on the stove.

—Well, now Maggie, no one would make out as how she could be confused with a mess of collards. Looks and brains both, no way in hell she'd go fooling with the likes of Screenwire. Talk about ugly. Do you really reckon his mama wrapped his head with a piece of screen to keep the skeeters off and that's how he got all them freckles?

— I never believed it.

The men carry on, weaving the net needle with its cotton string delicately as any woman tatting silk into lace. The flynet, stretched on poles running the length of the yard, its wide mesh about six inches square, frames familiar scenes like a row of tintypes lined up on the mantel: the upturned boat, the net reels and rusted tar pot canted sideways, the patch of cattails that edges itself up to the yard, the sagging corner of the porch where they congregate of an evening to smoke their cheroots and spit tobacco. The men walk up and down the length of flynet, talking of women they couldn't catch or wouldn't want to, dreaming of the trout they could.

Gilly listens, and later trolls out her line of questions.

— Who is Maggie, has she outgrown her drawers. Did she get some new ones, can I meet her, is she my age, one whole hand plus a good start on the other, this many. Is she, Papa?

His answer might or might not have satisfied her.

— It's just a shortcut through the marsh, my darling. Time for bed. On with your nightgown. Here it is, where we folded it this morning, in the bottom drawer. See how it's narrow but deep, it must be Maggie's.

— Now let's make it Gilly's Drawer, and name a creek after me.

— You have a boat named for you, miss. That's enough, he says, pulling the covers up to her chin, turning to leave.

— Don't forget to say it, she says.

What he used to say to me, what he would have said to our boys: *All the love in the world, my darling. Goodnight.*

And so Gilly's tale can only make me wish for what might have been. If our boys had lived, Gil would have taught them every marsh island and salt pond and freshwater creek between Great Hill and the

Neck, Pleasant Bay to Stage Harbor and on down to Blue Bill Hole. They would have built a boat and named it the *Miss Blythe*, and together we would have explored, together we would have mapped our world. Yes, Gil would have loved our boys, given enough time—all our boys except Ezra.

THIRTEEN

I IMAGINE HER, THIS DAUGHTER NOT MINE, in the coming days, boarding the ship that will take her away to England and then North Africa, where the fighting is, where we're already losing a war we've only just declared. She's determined to go to Algeria, where she can make a difference, she thinks. The only women allowed near the front are nurses, she is only a Red Cross volunteer, but that hard fact will be no deterrent.

How will she get there. Say she makes it as far as Italy, working in a canteen, and suppose a Jeep arrives to take her and a fellow volunteer, a shapely blonde from New York, to a villa where three generals sit smoking cigars, feet propped on antiquities. They offer the girls a drink. The blonde says no. Gilly says yes. A cognac, or scotch whiskey if you have it. She's the one, the men later agree, talking over their idea, an experiment, sending a Red Cross volunteer to the front with the 77th Evac Tent Hospital, trailing Rommel. Can't drink, how the hell will she stand all the rest of it. Never liked bottle blondes anyway. The tall, lanky girl, we're agreed, then, she's the one.

Her uniform will turn as dull brown as the crusted mud of Oran, except in those few hard-earned creases still holding a crisp pleat of blue, or where smeared with dried blood. She will not mind wearing combat boots or washing her face in her helmet, but she will ask headquarters for a clean change of uniform. She will hand out toothbrushes, write letters wistful or fictive for the young men, shave their faces too tender for whiskers or wounds, strike matches and hold cigarettes steady against the tremble of lips not kissed.

I am too old to ache for her, or them.

— Gilly, why are you so determined to go to the front? I ask.

We're sitting in the garden, where she's idly rearranging the row of conchs outlining what was once a flowerbed but now is an elegant container for weeds.

— My father always wanted a boy. He was so old by the time I came along, sixty-nine, almost seventy, I guess he just decided to make the best of things.

She's been using the tip of a conch to draw stick figures in the sandy soil.

— But he had a boy. Two boys, in fact. Our two sons.

Her hand ceases drawing, leaving a stick figure without a head.

— That's not true. He said I was his one and only, his best boy. He wouldn't have lied to me.

— His whole life was a lie.

— I think you're the one who lies.

I take the conch from her hand, and with it, I point at the gate.

— Out.

She stands, erases the stick figures with her foot, and leaves without another word. This time I'm sure she's gone away for good.

No matter. Little does she know, it will be I who shall haunt her someday, so that when she closes her eyes the veined lids will become a tatted veil.

FOURTEEN

Two DAYS LATER, though it seems as if weeks have passed, Gilly is back at my door. Through the ruby sidelight, she appears to be holding a bouquet of red roses, but once she's inside, I see she's picked a handful of sea holly from my dune. I start to remark—A handful of prickles, this is your peace offering?—but instead I walk her into the kitchen and gesture at a vase.

There's a mist hanging over Nauset Beach. It's chilly enough for one of Gil's boatneck sweaters, moth holes tatted over with silk. Letting my skin show through like a winged camouflage, it feminizes the heavy weave of his sweater.

— Let's have a cup of hot tea, maybe with a splash of amaretto, I say. That is, if you're ready for me to begin again. For someone who came here wanting information, you've managed to do most of the talking.

— No I haven't, she says.

I let it go. She did bring flowers. Of a sort. She puts the kettle on while I get another of Gil's sweaters from the hook by the door. As she pulls it on, the crown of her dark hair curling up out of the sweater's ribbed neck, I expect it to be him, but no. Her skin, not his, gleams through the mended holes.

— So we were at the part where you've buried your fiancé and my papa is sad. Is that about right? Gilly asks.

Sad. And yet. He's, she's come back. I catch myself, steer back to the story at hand.

— Yes, Gil is sad, I say. The worst kind of sad. The kind that has anger at its core.

— I understand that.

Perhaps she'll make it to the front after all.

Both Gil's father and mine had asked, why not tutor Gil? He needs steadying. As if conjugating Latin verbs by rote could ever be a cure for his contagion: books flung from shelves, their splayed covers floating on the richly patterned sea of an oriental carpet. Clipper ships in glass bottles crushed with a ball-peen hammer, splinters and shards ground into dents as big as half-dollars in the black walnut nightstand set between two beds. A flag no longer neatly folded, but ripped and burned and thrown in ashy tatters onto the stinking offal pile down at the wharf, sparking the gulls upward in a white spiral of tilt and scream, though not loud enough to muffle the cry retched up out of a single tortured throat.

I politely declined. It wasn't the waterspout of emotion that spun through Ben and Gil's room and left it a shambles. It wasn't that Ben's little brother was sixteen and I was twenty-four. Nor was it what we unwillingly shared between us—my fiancé—his brother—the man whose death cut us both adrift. Something else made me uneasy, unseated my soul. Perhaps even then, I knew to question who would be teacher, and what subjects taught.

FIFTEEN

IF GIL WAS FLOTSAM WRECKED BY BEN'S DEATH, I was jetsam, unneeded cargo thrown overboard, washed high above the tide line and left half buried in the wrack. No one bothered to notice that my life had stopped, that I lacked the dignity of being a war bride, much less a war widow. Who was there to notice, then, when I took off Ben's ring? When I rowed into the channel and shipped the oars? There was no one to notice when I wove a yellow-gold lock of his hair, along with a strand of mine, through the gold band, so that it shone bright as Rumpelstiltskin's lost bargain. I was the only one to see it turn and glint as I held it out over the gunnel and then released it. Only I was there to watch a wave reach out to finger it, and then let it go.

— That's just the saddest ever.

— Well. What else was there to do. You fall in love. You'd better be able to fall out.

— How did my mother fall in love? Gilly asks.

Under my breath, I use one of my best curses. But she will not see me ruffled.

— I thought you came here to ask questions about your father.

— Well I did, but that was before I knew there was a you, she says.

Fair enough, I think.

I feel like a traitor to myself, speaking of Maud O'Neal—I won't say Lodge—in my own house.

— Get my slicker. Let's walk down by the cliff.

The rain has left clouds spread across the horizon like soggy bed ticking, alternating stripes of white and gray. They seep rain every now and then, and humidity blankets the air, ready to wring out more. But there's plenty of time to say whatever I have to say about *her*.

— All right, I say. Keep up the pace. You walk like an old woman.

She laughs, and taking giant steps, she passes me and turns to walk backward, arms clasped behind her back.

— You may well wonder where I got my notions about your mother after only one meeting. But I know Gil. And from the brief time I was able to observe the twelve-year-old Maud O'Neal, the paucity of her life, and the size of her ambitions, I know her as well.

This is what I think the future Mrs. Lodge must have told herself.

I stop to empty sand from my shoes. Gilly kicks hers off too. Dash retrieves one, nudges her hand. She throws it. Honestly, I don't know why I bother. But then she says Go on. So I do.

Miss Anna Maud O'Neal will say—say, not simper—I don't see her as the simpering type. Obliging? Earnest? Yes, that will be just about right.

Miss O'Neal, then, will say:

— Mr. Lodge. Don't you want me to catch some bait for you? How'm I doing with the cast net? It's better, don't you think, when I put more of my body into it? Let my shoulders twist right up out of my waist? Look, my arms near about make a circle so the net'll hit the water full out.

Our handsome Yankee, he'd just nod, that's if you're lucky. But that's all right, it'd be good enough, it's all I need to turn a raised eyebrow into a full-blown conversation. If I'd only seen then that I was talking to myself.

I had to make do. Otherwise I would've had to sit there in dead silence. Instead, I got good at interpreting, just like it was a foreign language. I could turn his squint into paragraphs, if not pages, of the most fascinating discussion. A turn of his body ten degrees toward me was as good as a marriage proposal. All to be parsed with my best friend, Garnet.

— Mr. Lodge personally asked me to catch baitfish for him, went so far as to say as how a bucketful of finger mullet caught by my own hand, my own delicate hand, is what he said, that'll be his good luck charm for some puppy drum. Me, his good luck charm! He says I have great form when I throw the cast net. He says the way I turn from the waist, and the way I keep good and loose, lets the energy move out from my shoulders and down the length of my arms, he says I have such slender, graceful arms, and he says how I release the net just at the right point, it lets the net sail out in a perfect circle— that's how I can always get all the baitfish he needs.

Garnet is fascinated, or jealous, or both.

— My. He is really looking at you, watching your every move, she says.

With a knowing smile I duck my chin, as if to say, Yes, isn't it wonderful?

I was so busy figuring out what he might be thinking that I never really asked him much about himself. Maybe because he'd always been there, just around. Sure, that first year caused some talk, the winter of the telegram, saying his people up North were looking for him. That was when he helped out on that rescue, shot the line right out to the ship, first try, and my papa caught him out, put two and two together, said you're not who you say you are. Even if they did give him points for humor, calling himself Mr. Dodge instead of Cap'n Lodge. Well, that was grown-up business that didn't signify, nothing to do with me. I was just a girl, same as being invisible. He was a man. So when he showed up again the next year, I lumped him in the same category as my father and the other men at the station, important, other things on their minds.

When he first came to Chicamacomico, I was happy living in my pretend world. Switching my leg with a reed to make myself gallop, I could manage to be horse and rider all at the same time. I was always someone or something else, someplace else. That was the true me, the whole world, all at once.

So our Yankee captain sat around at the station with the men, talking or working on the surfboat or holding Queen's hoof to pry a shell loose while one of the men brought the cart around to take the Lyle gun down to the beach for a practice drill.

When the men gathered on the porch after dinner, he always joined them. When the Canadas started veeing in for the winter, he'd go off with the men to cut brush for the blinds. He was just around. And then come springtime he'd be gone. It seemed natural as the geese migrating—what was there to ask? In my life, things come and go: the tides, the birds, the spring run of blues, they give way to red drum every fall. I never asked where they went, neither him nor the fish. Mr. Gil Lodge was just another thing the tide brought in.

That is, until the fifth season, when all of a sudden he weren't just another change of the weather. He was somebody to compare with the boys who'd come hanging around for the taffy pulling, and how could a bunch of boys, with their wispy sideburns and moustaches faint as a faded tan, ever hope to compete? He was a man. And he was looking at me.

So, our talks, pass the salt please, weather's fairing off, night sleep tight, Gracie's pulling at the bit give her her head, moved from polite conversation into code for take this from my fingers, meet me for a sail, I see you in my dreams, ride like the wind, come find me.

Yes he was courting me, or at least he was courting something. In looking back, I wonder if I was just his way of laying claim to a place he loved, a way of living in it.

He said Will you. And I said Yes.

Gilly throws the shoe. She doesn't look at me.

— That's all right, I say. Go on. Come back this afternoon. If you feel like it.

— How can you stand it?

I don't answer. What's there to say? We walk back to the edge of the cliff where we left the other shoes. At first she doesn't notice I've put hers on.

— That's how, I guess.

I walk away.

— No, don't stop, not yet, she says.

Ah, but my mind, it never stops. Yet how is Gilly to know that, unless there's been talk around town—You *do* know, dear, that woman, Blythe Lodge, she's more than a little crazy, just like her husband, and who's to say which of them sent the other off the deep end first?

But aren't we all on the edge of that precipice? What pressures must come to bear in any person's life to tip one overboard? How many years spent on the cusp between so-called normal and quaintly eccentric, before that final shove to full-on, moon-barking madness.

SIXTEEN

AFTER BEN DIED, the beach became my only respite. There's no better place to pine than on an empty shore, where one day is much like the next, with only yourself to quibble with or to question why. I would leave town and head east across Chatham Harbor to Nauset Beach, that long, thin strip of land outrigged in the ocean, marking the tenuous edge between a hulking continent and the sea's long reach. There at the margin of the world, I found a toilsome peace, all mine. Or so I thought.

My day was doled out, fifteen minutes at each turn of the tide, time enough to walk or wade, pole or row, my shallow-draft boat to the narrow strand that was sometimes an island and sometimes a barrier spit. This predictable rhythm, timed to the white clockface of the moon, clashed nicely with the vagaries of the wind. Though eventually the quarter hours would become a gamble I almost hoped I would lose.

For there was Gil, walking wind-drunk down the beach, more days than not. As though guided by inner compasses, we sailed clear of one another. Out of respect, out of fear—of what?

There came a day when I did lose the gamble, misjudged the tide; whether I did so on purpose, I can't say. It had already started to rain and the wind was shoving at my back. Gil must have recognized me, despite—or who knows, because of—my attire: Father's linen shirt and canvas hunting jacket hanging loosely, and sailcloth britches worn soft as chamois, stuffed inside a pair of gumboots. Gil was standing with his face to the wind, and so there was nowhere to escape his gaze on the empty strand.

— Blythe, he said. Miss Harding.

A rising tide floats all boats, I thought. Why not see where it carries us?

— I was just about to leave my calling card. I've always wanted a tour of your house.

— I think you've had one already, he said.

SEVENTEEN

I HAD HEARD STORIES—who hadn't—about Gil's Folly, or Whale Manor, or whatever people liked to call it, the beach shanty Gil had built just before the war. Ben had provided an extra pair of hands, but it was all Gil's design; in fact, Ben was loath to claim any part of it.

Ben had told me how Gil wanted his shanty to be invisible, but on this flat beach, horizontal as a carpenter's spirit level, he would've needed to take up residence in a sand fiddler's hole. Not invisible, then, but well camouflaged, it rose out of the sand as though conjured by earth, air, and sea. It flew and swam and reared up into a heap almost anyone would agree was unfit for habitation.

Each day, Ben had given me a report. Gil, he said, insisted on ships' timbers as studs, which was not so unusual; but then came the arcing bones of a whale's girth as roof trusses. Ben suggested cedar brush or shingles for the siding, but Gil said no, the one too temporary, the other too like town.

Instead he covered both roof and walls with all manner of flotsam smoothed and tinted by the sand, so that the shanty seemed like something the ocean might have hammered together, if it had thought to fasten tight its dredged-up treasures rather than scatter them. So there were shingles, yes, but also gulls' wings tucked into the walls, and wadded net and bits of canvas and broken hatch covers and the sieved jaw of a baleen whale chinked tight with krill.

The two brothers hoisted a large strip of whale skin onto the roof, its chimney-sized blowhole, shriveled and leathered by the elements, spouting smoke now, not sea. The roof itself was shingled over with tails and fins, dorsals and pectorals, overlapping like outsized fish scales. The windows were made from the eye sockets of a sperm whale, glass cut to fit and glinting like spectacles, a way to see out of, or into, the deeps of a boy's imagination.

Ben was not to know that his brother's secret dreamings were a place I would someday yearn to lose myself in; that I would beggar my soul for the chance to caress each jagged, brilliant thought, polish it smooth, and set it on my finger like a promise.

Poor, unwitting Ben. It was he who first told me of his brother's makeshift mansion, how it reeked, how skillfully it was engineered, as Gil built it wing by bone, ripe with rotting bits of flesh. Perhaps, then, I can claim it was indeed Ben who put a second ring on my finger and not I who proposed to Gil.

The day I first saw Gil's Folly, it was bleached clean by the sun, white as a skull, intricate as lace tatting. I explored its fabled dimensions, now with drifted sand packing its foundations like mortar, so that the shanty was of the beach, not on it. When its occasional feathered wing lifted in the wind, it seemed no more out of place than a gull or a tern that had breasted a shallow nest in the sand.

It was from this shanty that Gilead Lodge ventured out into his days, walked restless into his solitary nights. I can't say exactly when we stopped heading in opposite directions, exactly when our courses veered parallel, then intersected, as we groped our way by dead reckoning. Of course there were those who said I well knew what course I had set, a headlong collision my intention all along. He, at least, they said, was innocent of the depth of my currents, blind to the direction of my winds, unaware that any errant wave can capsize a life, taking the full breadth of the ocean to crest and roll.

EIGHTEEN

SO IT BEGAN. That first encounter, we, or he, talked about Ben, for hours. Gil spoke slowly but with authority, calculating Ben, adding up all his virtues, subtracting none of his failures, even his ultimate failure to still be alive on this earth. Telling me what Ben was good at. Reading. And understanding. Not just books and poetry, he said, but wind and water, and how the angle of an oar could get you from one side of Pleasant Bay to the other without draining the life out of you. How Ben would ramble on, about Archimedes' principle and angular displacement and the Bernoulli effect, which, if he recalled accurately, was something about how the pressure exerted by a fluid decreases as its velocity increases, which was so much gibberish until Ben explained what it had to do with how fast Gil could get from town to his island camp, depending on how fast the tide was running, and then Ben took on an aura of wizard, genius, alchemist—more, so much more, than big brother, or mother, darling Ben.

Gil's words came at a whisper, as the rain tumbled and thrummed and pelted the roof of his Linnaean castle, and the smoke of his fire spiraled up and out of the living, breathing hole where the sea once spumed, and soon every crease in my salt-stiffened clothes was steamed smooth. The single room was small, rimmed with shelves.

We sat on his one nod at luxury, an old Turkey carpet spread atop a thick mat of eelgrass to pad the uneven floorboards. Our backs rested against whalebone or the ribs of ships. Our bare feet touched and then quickly drew apart, boots left by the door and upended to let the water drain.

Gil told how Ben was forever taking the blame for things he himself, willful or unwitting, had done, how Ben never allowed him to shoulder any of the punishment, be it stacking cordwood or cleaning out the henhouse. Ben grimaced at every filthy leaf or chicken feather or crumpled daddy longlegs that stuck to his clothing, while Gil was ready to thrust them under his magnifying glass or glue them to the edge of his lampshade.

Gil spoke as though his brother were someone I had never met. And in many ways, this was true, for how people know one another is imperfect and refracted.

NINETEEN

GILLY AND I HAVE ESTABLISHED A RHYTHM TO OUR DAYS. Coffee on the porch in the mornings, then she returns in time for a walk on the beach and a cognac, or on blow days, we wrap up in blankets and sit in the lee of the porch, moving from chair to hammock to chair as the storm dictates.

Just as I have wondered how Gilly sees me, does she wonder how I see her? Is it a matter of youth that they see only *Them* and *Us*, that they can be so sure this will never happen to them? But then, I have always seen many lives walking around in one body, as though I could see shadows clinging tight. I look and see a child, the outline of a six-foot-tall man looming outsized around his toddler-sized body. In a passing stroller, I see an old man, baby fat plumping his whiskered sunken cheeks.

And so when I look at Gilly, her narrow, bright face, crystalline blue eyes inquisitive above angular cheekbones, the face of a young woman flush with life, I also see the same eyes large, unblinking, in a small rounded face peached with flawless skin, lips parted across tiny pearled teeth. I see rheumed eyes small in their bony sockets. A rune of a face with its crosshatching of deep grooves and fine lines. A parenthetical smile, gums receding from teeth yellowed as a scrimshawed whalebone, what was once a beauty mark at the corner of her mouth now a mole sprouting a single coarse hair.

Unnerving, this trickery, so that when I look at someone it's like seeing time melting and congealing, years falling away to reveal smooth pink skin, years piling on, folding and creasing, skin leathered by too much wear. I have to blink hard to bring into focus what I gather is the Gilly appropriate to this moment. But if my mind drifts, I can believe her child or crone.

I can call to mind any of these visages of embodied time, with anyone I meet. Anyone except Gil. Him I could only see with a singular gaze, hyperfocused. I could never see enough of him, my eyes dying of thirst for the sight of him. What he might have looked like with wisped hair fine as a baby's breath, what he might one day look like with hair grizzled as dried seaweed, this I could never see—only the man before me, so vital, even in repose.

And what of my little ones? Can I summon an image of youth or middle age from their infant faces? No, not for my twins, whom I never laid eyes on while they yet breathed.

TWENTY

COD FISHING IN SPRING, shorebird hunting in summer, shooting geese and swan and ducks in the fall, wrecking all winter. Most said Gil Lodge was lazy or spoiled, some even said he wasn't all there, only had one oar in the water, that boy. He should just ship out, others said. Take a Nantucket sleigh ride for a year or three. Or circle the entire globe. Why not? A few years on a China clipper would set him aright.

I knew what he needed. To go south, to Carolina. To search for a battleground, a grave, an old soldier's recollection, something to mark Ben's passing from this life to the next. Only this, I thought, would set him free.

He said he would build a boat to take him there, to the place on the map marked Chicamacomico, just north of Cape Hatteras, latitude 35º 35' 44.5" N, longitude -75º 27' 58.7" W, numbers he carried in his head and idly wrote out in the sand with a bit of oyster shell or carved with his clasp knife into the stained and rutted table where he ate his meals. I would sometimes come across those numbers, Ben's final bearings, where Gil had scrawled them with his stub of a carpenter's pencil in the margins of whatever book he was reading.

He said he would go. He would build the boat he and Ben had designed, spending hours on their hands and knees lofting the flared hull they thought would be more seaworthy in the shallow waters of the bays and sounds. He would sew his own sails, stoke the fire and hammer a pair of oarlocks out of hot iron, he would fell his own mast. But first the oars.

Fine, I said, but must you encompass the entirety of a maritime forest in your mind's eye, when all you're doing is making two oars?

His answer, if he'd bothered to acknowledge the question, was to spend five days selecting and yet another half day felling a perfectly matched pair of white ash trees. I watched as he hewed them down to where the growth rings were flattest. The wood curled beneath the spokeshave as he thinned each oar's blade and faired the corners with the block plane. Ben's formula for a properly balanced loom was pinned above the workbench but Gil preferred to feel his way like a blind man along the length of a once-living tree, his drawknife coaxing the tree into an extension of his own arm, the diameter of the oar's shaft no greater than the circle made by his thumb and forefinger. Close attention to the faint grain of the wood that replicated the whorls of his fingertips, a steady fixation on the fine hairs of his arms now furred with sawdust flying from his rasp, allowed him to look without seeing, think without remembering.

TWENTY-ONE

THAT YEAR, IT WOULD HAVE BEEN 1866, when Gil wasn't building a boat, he was building a reputation. Sportsmen from Boston and New York sought him out as a guide; asked if he would let his dog, Dash, sire puppies; wanted to buy his decoys; asked for his recipes for salt duck and goose-blood pudding. In town, though, most people thought hunting was Gilead Lodge's poor excuse for doing what he felt like and not much else.

To my mind, the townspeople resented his popularity as a hunting guide, young as he was. Didn't like that his decoys went for a higher price than the old-timers'. And they thought spending hours fiddling with dead birds was just plain strange.

Between the shorebirds in spring and summer and waterfowl in fall and winter, he knocked together four seasons dedicated to observing, shooting, plucking, and cooking anything with feathers and a beak or bill. He was never wasteful. He ate or gave away or sold whatever he shot, except for a few birds that somehow spoke to him.

His favorite thing to do in a northeaster—other than to be out in it, alive to it, arms outstretched like some crazed weathervane, buffeted by wave upon wave of wind whose direction was made visible with his every spin and turn—was to sit at his workbench, bird in hand, the wind's whistling a birdsong.

I kept my promise to sit quietly, a book propped in my lap as a foil against his command not to stare at him. Then I could secretly look my fill at his dark head bent over a limp bird, seeing his brows narrow in concentration as he coaxed the thin fabric of skin from the bird's airy bones, eider down and pin feathers smoothed into place. Careful not to let one of the sharp quills puncture the skin, he draped the feathered cloak over a hand-whittled frame. His workbench was a nest of wood shavings.

I asked him why he chose such close, delicate work for stormy nights, when the shanty creaked like Noah's own ark, breathy with animal cries and insect thrum, bird whistle and reptilian hiss.

— The wind concentrates my mind, he said.

So the birds that had one by one fallen from the sky in a fluid co-alescence of aim, reaction, and timing now stood or flew or preened on his shelves, currents of sand washing the birds' feet. The flaring shadows and ruffled feathers turned a still life into a covey of birds intent on that urgent whisper calling them to trust some faraway shore. Winging air or water, they would move, restless in the storm.

Somehow, then, news of his birds, sculpted from their own feathers, moved through town and beyond. He turned down other hunters' requests with a simple no, I only do my own birds, but when I pressed him, why not make money, you could name your price, he would recite a litany of excuses: the men spoiled the birds with the inaccuracy of their shot; the gauges of their guns were too large or too small; the birds, jostled in the game bag or tossed carelessly into the well of the boat, were mangled; their dogs were hard-mouthed, dropping a wad of feathers at their feet. Neither would he sell his own willets or sanderlings or godwits or avocets to the hunters who wanted to set them under glass domes in their libraries back in Boston or Providence.

On those occasions when the wind and tide helped my journey across Chatham Harbor, I would arrive at the shanty and check my bearings. Licking my finger, I would hold it up, finding that sure spot where all wetness evaporates, sucked dry by the wind. North or northeast, southerly or westerly, it never mattered. The birds would be standing on their shelves where he had arranged them, all facing into the wind. Each visit, they multiplied, and I would look at them, my eyebrows raised, as they crowded themselves wing to wing like birds on a wire. Never mind what price they would fetch, he said. His birds would not be caged.

It was that undercurrent of arrogance that was somehow attractive, that made you think you could outstroke it, even when you knew the current was going the wrong way, a one-way trip out to sea.

TWENTY-TWO

GIL LEFT IN THE SUMMER. It was nearly winter when he returned, his seventeenth birthday marked, how? Up early, blowing on the embers of a driftwood fire before breaking camp alongside a marsh somewhere between Virginia and Maryland's Eastern Shore? A week later, where was he, the day I turned twenty-five? Doubtless, for someone his age, too high a number to contemplate, if he remembered my birthday at all.

And so we circled, going through the motions of our days like two deluded moths, blinded by the ritual of flame. He added a room to his shanty and turned his hand to larger birds. Over the bed, a whistling swan spread its wings like a downy canopy. The bedposts were carved oak from scavenged timbers, the slender necks of two swans entwined in a bird embrace. A quilt held bits of Gil's clothes and some shirts I remembered of Ben's. Its stitches were neat as a schoolgirl's sampler but the unbleached cotton was rough and the wide wales of corduroy were worn flat. The faded blue of a regimental flag was vivid in an otherwise monochrome counterpane. Gil's handiwork lay spread beneath the swan, the quilt billowy with eiderdown. There were two pillows. These things I took for a sign.

Gil worked at his bench in the dim winter light, alternating between practical tasks such as carving net needles and pouring lead pellets into rows of brass shells, and working on his new project, seagoing birds such as fulmars and petrels and shearwaters that seldom come ashore. About his trip, he said nothing.

One mild day in January, I helped him hang a seine net that needed repair. As we worked on opposite sides along the length of tarred cotton mesh, cutting out tangled strands and reknotting gaping holes, I imagined the net suspended from its cork floats, felt the current rippling down its length as Gil hauled it hand over hand into the dory, bubbles clinging along the four-inch squares of mesh like dewdrops pearled on a spider's web. A school of sea trout flowed beneath the boat and all along the net's reach. The tiny bubbles of air were as good as a solid wall, for the fish would not swim past them, out through the net's gaping holes. Something insubstantial as a bubble became solid as a prison bar, holding the fish bunched tight against the net, so that they became their own jailers.

We're no better than fish, I thought. How easy to find obstacles where there are none, locking ourselves inside our own inconsequential thoughts.

I started to share my reflection with Gil, since if there was silence to be filled, I was ever the one to fill it. But then he began, as though I had asked him. The words carried us along the length of net, then for a long walk down the beach and back, swept us into the shanty, through the careful building of a fire slow to start and down into the orange heat and blue flame of salt-cured wood turning cinder and ticking softly as it consumed itself, exhaling smoke.

He told, so that I could picture every sweep of oar and every starry night, of his journey south, and what he found there, or did not find.

Twined through the starts and stops and the circling back were long spells of quiet, the cracking of knuckles, pacing, a fist through the wall. When his disjointed story was ended came the first beautiful unraveling beneath the wings of the swan, its neck outstretched in full flight.

TWENTY-THREE

DID I SAY AS MUCH TO GILLY? Why not, if it pleases me.

Today we've taken the skiff out and are anchored back of Monomoy. What I have to tell next will best be illustrated by the blank stretch of beach before us.

— We'll be visiting Hatteras Island in our mind's eye. Do you remember Bannister O'Neal?

— No, he died before I was born, she says. But my poppy, Griffin, that's my grandfather, he used to talk about his dad, and I know what he looked like—his portrait's in the house at Chicamacomico.

She trails one hand in the water and with the other shades her eyes.

— Ready? I ask.

I think she likes hearing about the Banks better than she does Cape Cod. Maybe picturing the familiar through someone else's eyes is better than picturing something new. At any rate, she has the dreamy look of a child with a favorite storybook. No happy endings here, I start to say, but I keep silent. She can be the judge.

Suppose, then, it was a cool October day when Gilead Lodge walked off the beach at Chicamacomico and into Bannister O'Neal's ramshackle house capsized halfway between ocean and sound. Say it was the first, the only house he saw, and that stepping over the threshold felt like walking into the camp of the enemy.

— So. You've come looking for your brother's final resting place. The old man shook his head.

— No rest here, that's for damn certain. Anyway, doubt you'll find it. For years we'd come upon pieces of skeletons picked apart by an osprey or an otter out yon there in the marsh. Weren't much to bury, sure not enough to warrant hunting up two sticks to bind with a bit of twine and shove 'em crossways in the sand, never mind carving RIP. Still, have a sit-down. I can tell by the looks of you, we'll not be shut of you that easy.

Gil was at the end of his journey from Cape Cod to Cape Hatteras, his hands callused by weeks of hauling sail and pulling oars, one finger for each of the ten states whose splayed coasts he had outlined for hundreds of miles. He'd slogged the last fifteen on foot, the sparkling beach an unlikely battleground. The name of the battle, the Chicamacomico Races, seemed a flippancy, an atrocity, unpronounceable in its absurd jumble of vowels and consonants, and for those reasons, unforgettable.

Once the door closed behind Gil, the salt-stained windows doused the bright day. He started to strike a match, but then saw that the oil lamp's wick was nearly dry. Just as well. He wasn't sure he could have held the match steady.

Hard rowing is apt to make a man's hands tremble. That's what he hoped the men would think. The paper crackled when he tried to smooth the pages on his knee. He could always recite Ben's letter from memory. The lines blurred as he chanced quick looks at the two men who could have been carved from a single block of wood and left out to weather. The old man's face was runneled. His son already bore the marks of storm. A third man sat canted over in the far corner of the room.

For a moment Gil thought: *Ben.* But the disembodied head and chest were only the deadwood remnants of a man, a figurehead chiseled from a once-living tree, salvaged from some wrecked ship. An ill-fated ship, she must have been, to set a man and not a woman at her prow.

Now that he was here, Gil doubted he would find much consolation. Ben, peaceable Ben, gone off to war with the Massachusetts regiment, and for what? Ben who never hunted or fished with his younger brother because he couldn't stand the way a crippled brant's eye clouded over when you wrung his neck, who mourned the bright colors as they fled from a dying fish. He had a soft heart, soft hands, and marched off as though he were headed to an ordinary life-saving drill instead of away to a brutal war.

Gil's hands no longer shook. Still, he couldn't manage to find his way out of the silence that seemed to be these men's natural element. No matter. In his own good time, Bannister O'Neal began to speak. The wind had picked up, and Gil had to lean closer to hear him.

Bannister told how he and his oldest son, Henry, only the day before the battle, had hauled their boat, hull-side up, onto blocks. The next morning they'd begun scraping barnacles off the bottom, busy getting the *Alma View* ready for a new coat of paint, their minds on the fall run of red drum, the mainlanders' war nothing to do with them, until he and all his family found themselves crouched beneath her hull, not sure whether to stay or run.

— The closest the Rebs could come in was near-about two miles— the sound's mighty shallow out there. They waded about three-quarters of a mile, the water up to their middles, and then they opened fire at the Yanks lined up on the beach. All's we could see was blue legs heading south. Once they come past, we thought it was over.

— Before we could crawl out from under the boat, here come some more. This time it was gray legs, they had finally waded ashore. They come running up the beach and then back down, first the blue legs and then the grays, then back again, and that Mosquito Fleet circling away out there in the sound, little bitty boats that carried a sting, them great big old guns booming.

— Then we begun to realize our neighbors were running by, and Sally, she whispered to me she could recognize them, every one, by their calico skirts and the homespun of their trousers. Some slaves from off island that had swum here to freedom, we watched their black legs fly past, the soles of their feet pale as a flounder's bottom. They was all mixed in with the Rebs and the Yanks, and them horses' shanks pegging away in the sand.

The old man reached for a tintype in a crisscrossed frame of carved driftwood, held it to the watery light, and then set it down.

— It was some race, all right. 'Cept races have a winner, don't they?

Gil cleared his throat, hesitated, picked up Ben's letter again. The tremor returned, but somehow it no longer mattered. He read aloud:

If our hunger were a physical ache, our thirst was something else, a veritable madness. You will recall, Dear Brother, Coleridge's mariner in agony, water everywhere, and while we, too, had the sea rolling at our feet, so tantalizing, and the Pamlico within trudging distance, yet neither a drop could we drink.

As the words flowed on, he pictured not the stubborn miles he'd just walked, through sand, marsh, and black clouds of mosquitoes, from Chicamacomico to Hatteras and back, in replication of Ben's battle or race or whatever he might have called it. Instead he felt the wet towel snapped against bare back, saw the volume of poetry tucked under his pillow, the leaf or feather glued to the lampshade, the native language of two boys. He heard the shouts, the brothers' voices tumbling over one another as they filched the forbidden Chartreuse from their father's sideboard, not lime green, not lemon yellow, no, not even the sublime yellow-green of his prized shooter, a four-vaned cat's-eye marble, but a curse-worthy monkey-snot green or putrid pea-vomit green or custard-yellow leper's pus, Ben laughing, even taking a swig, and yet when they looked up to see their father standing over them, smacking the empty bottle in his hand, Ben claimed he'd drunk it all, every drop.

The old man's chair scraped the floor. A series of gusts carried a gull's cry, lifting it octaves higher on the wind. Gil heard none of it, all sound suspended.

Sand sieved through the rafters and trickled out through holes drilled in the floorboards to release the occasional hurricane tide. The house sat like an hourglass upended. With a tilt of the wrist, past and present could intermingle, sand flowing back and forth between the curved glass chambers.

Gil didn't notice whether the O'Neals were even listening. He continued, half reading, half reciting from the letter a Union soldier had found in a rucksack left on a knob of cedar driftwood, placed there by Ben's own hand or by the wind.

For some fifteen miles I skirted the Sound, and all along the shore, in every sulfurous mud flat and marshy swale, men were lying, no wounds visible, unless you credit salt-crusted sunburn and the overlap of mosquito bites like fish scales, and eyes blank as a dead man's. I have witnessed soldiers bleeding out their lives in the dirt still summon the energy to thrust a letter out to me as though I were God's own messenger and I could fly away home to deliver it, or them. Yet these men, my men, had not even the strength to lift a finger. The enemy's vessels were now nearly abreast, but when I tried to urge the men onward, they would whisper between cracked lips that they did not care. So utterly hopeless, they would murmur, "Go and leave me here to die."

Gil turned to the next page, but everyone knew the way the story ended. He folded the letter and put it back in his pocket. For a time, the only sound was the faint boom of the sea.

— So there's no graveyard? Gil asked.

All this time, John Patrick O'Neal had continued to sit in the corner with his chair cocked back on two legs. Gil guessed Bannister's son was five or six years older than himself, twenty-two or perhaps twenty-three.

The two O'Neal men exchanged glances.

John Patrick let the chair drop to the floor, turned it to sit straddled, arms draped over the ladderback, and shrugged.

— There was a graveyard, down the Banks.

Gil looked at him as if to say, Well? Tell me. It's what I came here for.

John Patrick pivoted up and crossed to the door. Opening it, he leaned against the jamb and looked away, framed in the reflected sheen off Pamlico Sound.

Gil felt eyes boring into his back and turned to look at the inanimate half-man propped in the corner. In the sudden light, it looked less like Ben, could have been this man's brother. In John Patrick O'Neal he saw the same brow, rough-hewn, bringing out the blue of his eyes, the finely chiseled nose, cheeks two smooth planes, hair sawcut, the sun-bleached tips spiked and whorled by the wind.

So perhaps not a ship's figurehead then, but a sculpture. The nicks in John Patrick's hands not from shucking oysters but from a carving knife, whittling the likeness of his elder brother, not lost at sea in some freak storm, but fallen in battle, if defending your family huddled under a boat in your backyard could be called a battle.

When John Patrick began to speak, his lips barely moved. He told how he'd been gigging for flounder down there on the cape one night, near a scarp cut by a storm, a cliff of dry sand overhanging the wrack line. That's when he'd come upon the wooden boxes that at first he took for half-buried cargo. Like all islanders he'd heard stories of hidden treasure, and he and his younger brother Griffin had even found a few trinkets themselves.

In the lantern light, he saw through gaps in the planks what at first appeared to be tiny stars, or gems, or something, he couldn't say what, so many neatly spaced, glittering rows of light, each light about the size of a match head.

A wave caught him from behind, buckling his knees, and then sluiced through the half-rotted wood, making a peculiar chirring sound. He leaned over and used the iron tip of his gig to pry open one of the lids and then thrust his hand inside. As he held the lantern up, the low hum ratcheted higher, a crescendo of controlled frenzy. He realized it was not ship's cargo, not diamonds or stars or the sea's phosphorescence, not anything but the gleaming eyes of row upon row of tree frogs or spring peepers, he never knew which, huddled inside what he now realized were coffins.

He dropped lid, gig, and lantern, and sprinted into the receding tide, taking up great handfuls of sand, scrubbing his arms to the elbows. He said that if only he could, he would scour his mind clean of the sight that still gave him nightmares, frogs clamped like green barnacles to the gleaming skull and all down the loose bones and cascade of ribs clattering in the ocean's wash.

John Patrick pushed himself back from the doorframe and in two steps he was off the porch, headed for the landing. He flung himself into his skiff and shoved off. Gil stood immobile as the hastily raised sail caught the breeze and flapped in unison with the lapping water, underscoring the memory of his brother's voice reciting from *The Ancient Mariner* the lines:

> *The many men, so beautiful!*
> *And they all dead did lie:*
> *And a thousand thousand slimy things*
> *Lived on; and so did I.*

TWENTY-FOUR

GIL STUMBLED OUT AND IN JUST A FEW STRIDES *had walked the length of the weather-drubbed* house whose back was turned to the ocean.

He was surprised to find Bannister following him, and though all he wanted was to be left alone, he waited for the old man to make his way through the clotted sand down to the wave-tamped beach. They stood at the surf's edge for some time without speaking, looking out at the dozens of sailing vessels, barks, barkentines, square-riggers, and schooners, two-, three-, and four-masted. The ships' masts clustered like a grove of trees with the wind moving through them, and like trees, the vessels seemed rooted to the spot, yet what was holding them there, far from harbor or landing?

Bannister pitched his slow drawl just above the level of the surf and pointed southeast. There, the peculiar confluence of competing winds and tides wrestled the cape, moving and shaping it, pinning unwary ships on Diamond Shoals.

— When the wind blows from any southerly direction, vessels come in, just there, at Kinnakeet Anchorage, he said. The ships—leastways those with captains who know these waters—they furl their sails and wait, for days or even weeks, until the wind turns out of the north or nor'west. Otherwise, they can't build up enough speed, and they find themselves caught smack between the warm waters of the north-beating Stream and the Labrador's cold south'ard flow.

Gil stood picturing the Atlantic's two mighty rivers, one long as a continent, the other crossing an ocean, and the fragile headland of the cape sloping down into the sea, with only a change in color, blue to gray, marking the infamous shoals. No wonder this was known as the Graveyard of the Atlantic. That the waters off Cape Cod were called the same did not seem so strange, a kind of destiny.

— For every ship you see out there, there's another ten sunk to the bottom. Some six hundred of them, along with countless lost souls, said the old man. If you're not careful, son, you'll find yourself adrift between those two currents, north and south, and like all the rest, you're sure to wreck.

Bannister reached up, put his hand on Gil's shoulder, and gave it a squeeze.

— Set your sails and get on with it.

He turned and made his way back up the strand.

Before Gil lay the hard-packed sand beach with nothing to interrupt it for as far as he could see, what Bannister had called the most beautiful natural racetrack in the world, the Chicamacomico and Kinnakeet Flats, where on Sundays, islanders rooted for any horse they thought could beat Jesse Thomas Gray's roan stallion. In Gil's mind it would never be a racecourse, filled with cheers and laughter, but neither was it a battlefield or a graveyard, simply a vast emptiness.

In minutes, tide and wind erased everything, no hoofprints, no footprints, nothing but a track of sand less than a mile wide and fifty miles long, unmoored from the continent thirty miles distant, which rolled westward for three thousand miles, and to the east, another three thousand miles of ocean.

Gil squinted hard. The sunlight's random glances off a belt buckle or a spyglass made the ships seem to flash in the distance as though signaling—what message? Send word. Please. How do I survive my own two furious currents, the salty undertow of blood running beneath my skin, pulling my heart hard against my ribs, the salt tears flowing like rip currents down my face? He lay down on the sand and became part of the glistening beach, his body stretched long like a razor clam, and then he curled inward on himself like a conch, his back to the world.

He thought of taking a shell and writing an epitaph, rest in peace, Ben's name, something, to show he was here, had been here, was here still and always would be. But even as he lay there, the sand sheeted and swirled as the wind moved it into new patterns, until the part in his dark hair, the creases in his clothes, the folds of his skin were stitched with gold. Unseen, the constellations turned, their star patterns waiting until night to reveal themselves. The shoals moved, the inlets shifted, the stars wheeled. Nothing stayed the same.

He pressed his cheek into the sand, skewing his vision, and heard an incoming wave that seemed to sizzle from deep within the earth.

The sizzle turned to stampede, and in quick, bright flashes he saw the legs of the soldiers, blue and gray, as they marched or fled or fell, the panicked children churning sand, old men shoeless, women dragging burlap sacks in their wake, black ankles bearing the pink scarred imprint of chains, the legs of horses and the heels of riders digging into their flanks, a handsome man with blue eyes and whorled hair falling headlong onto the beach, and Ben.

He lay there for some time, then shoved up out of the trough the receding tide had dug around him, and headed back to the house. He would leave Ben's volume of Coleridge for John Patrick, and within, marking his brother's favorite passage, the telegram's tattered star.

Bannister took the book from him, briefly covering the younger man's hand with his own stiff fingers. He handed him a few provisions: salted herring, Hayman sweet potatoes, a refilled flask. He leaned against the net house, no expectation of a backward glance, took out his knife, and began whittling.

Gil headed north, his narrow footprints, widely spaced, becoming fainter in the distance, bare feet orchestrating a new refrain in the shush of deep sand.

TWENTY-FIVE

GILLY DOES NOT ASK: What was it like, then, for you to watch this story take shape on the lips of Ben's little brother? And I do not answer.

A thousand words, arranged just so, their sentences, their paragraphs, their pauses, do these add up to truth? Like dismantling a clock, looking for time. Where? In the pendulum, hypnotic in its smooth oscillation? In the clock's hands, fingers crossed at ten of ten, or five after one, hoping for what? In its wheels and cogs interlocking, do they bear the weight of time, measured how, in slow reeling inches? Is time only a matter of duration, or does it lie altogether outside the clock, an accumulation of synchronicities, the only thing that makes any one moment stand out in memory. *This* makes me think of *that*, an endless loop, this eternity of the mind. Dig through the sentences, all the words, the minutes and months—count them, conjugate them, weigh them, parse them. To discover what? That Ben could die, and yet Gil and I could live on. These two impossibilities, these immutable facts, became an irrelevance.

This I did not say, for if one has never experienced it, new love sprung from old, it would seem a sacrilege.

TWENTY-SIX

— ALL THESE BIRD JOURNALS, Gilly says one afternoon. I suppose they have a purpose, if you're just dying to know why a mockingbird sits in the grass and flashes its wings or something useful like that. Actually, why do they? Anyway, I like books, how they sweep you up, carry you off to some faraway place and drop you down at someone's dinner table. Which reminds me, what do you have to eat?

— There's a whole ocean full of fish right over there.

She rummages in the cupboard and comes back eating cranberry honey out of the jar, then walks to the bookcase and trails her sticky fingers along the rows of spines buckled by salt air. I could say something, but I don't interrupt, interested to see where she goes.

— Like this one. Who could hold another thought when taking this in? *Titus Andronicus*. Her own children, cooked up and served for dinner.

I've shelved Shakespeare next to the Brothers Grimm, how we consume, unawares, the things we love best.

— I would never want a stepmother, she says. They are always, always wicked.

Has she noticed my juxtaposition? I thought it quite nice, *Titus* next to *The Juniper Tree*.

— I could be your stepmother.

— No. I mean. You wouldn't be *that* kind of stepmother. You couldn't be, could you? The wicked ones, who always try to come between father and child. You're the opposite. You make me feel closer to him.

I watch her thinking. I know she's thinking of her mother, how she was competing, always competing with her own daughters, four all told, each in her own way edging out Gil's affections, but never equaling, how I want to believe it, never equaling me, lying there in the bed between them, I, more real to him than her own limbs stretched alongside.

Gilly draws another slim volume from the shelf. A Hemingway.

— Do you think I, could I please borrow this? she asks.

She opens the book, brings the splayed pages, freckled with water spots, to her face, breathes in, sighs.

— It smells like ocean, she says. Salt. Hot sun. Seaweed.

She hands me the book.

— See?

I close my eyes, bring the brittle yellowed pages to my face.

Salt. Sun. Seaweed. The amalgamation of these three, what the marsh has made of them, this, the essence of saltmeadow hay.

A few pale yellow straws fall from the book.

— Gil is forking salt hay. It's humid, the wind out of the southwest. The greenhead flies are biting. I walk in circles, tamping down the hay. I am a human baling machine, making more room in the loft. The sweat keeps rolling down my face, dripping onto the book. The sun is setting by the time we finish, by the time I turn the last page. 'We could have had such a damned good time together,' I say, quoting Brett from memory.

I close the book and hand it back to her.

She opens it to the last page, to Jake Barnes's reply.

— 'Yes. Isn't it pretty to think so?' she reads.

She looks at me, brave eyes, unpitying, a knowing look that needs bear no kindness, only truth. I am seen, through and through.

She nods. Puts the book under her arm. Pats Dash on the head.

— I'll be back.

I listen for the screened door to slam. I'm not disappointed.

TWENTY-SEVEN

WHAT WOULD IT HAVE BEEN LIKE IF BEN'S WAR had been here and not there, the fight at my doorstep, not theirs. I think, what if their dead were abandoned here or lost or left unshriven in our own marshes, far from home, and not only those who signed up for the fight.

This I wonder with Gilly sitting in my parlor, preparing to go to another faraway war. Could she bring to her mind's eye the wind-propped house by the sea, and does she see the old man and his son, the men who would lay out a path leading to her own birth? For they were Gilly's kin on her mother's side—Maud's grandfather, the sad and gentle old man, and Maud's uncle, the young man with the tortured memories. Bystanders in an uncivil war.

Who would Gilly meet in another war, on another front? And how might their lives intersect, she and her young men sure to be scarred by something—if not bullets or bombs or bayonets, then sights, sounds, smells, burdened with the unassuageable guilt of the not-dead.

She's paid close attention to the story of how, the year after Appomattox, her father had first come south to Hatteras Island, to Chicamacomico, to the house that at times leaned seaward and at times threatened to pitch-pole directly into Pamlico Sound. How she came to have two uncles on opposite sides of the war. And how the telegram's black star announcing her Uncle Ben's death came to be passed from her father to her Uncle John Patrick, whose brother Henry might very well have been the one who killed Ben. And if not, who most certainly wished him dead. Not him or any other man in particular, more the creed they represented, embodied in blue or in gray. The O'Neals held allegiance to neither, these men charging up and down the island not their home, interlopers among a place and a people who wanted nothing more than to be left alone.

— Why have I never heard of this battle, this Chicamacomico Races, or that my family had anything to do with it? she asks.

— They say history is written by the victors? It's a ridiculous name for a battle? I don't know why this well-thumbed story is a revelation, I answer.

I wonder, but do not ask, What else have they kept from you?

TWENTY-EIGHT

— I'm going to meet him, you know. In Paris.

— Ben? Jake Barnes? Gil?

I'm disoriented. So many wars. Looking at her, like looking at him.

A few moments pass before my eyes are able to shutter the image of him. Then she's back, a girl in an open-necked shirt, wrinkled, and trousers that clip her bare ankles, a slip of tan flashing between rolled-up cuffs and canvas shoes.

She's become accustomed to whatever's going on behind my eyes, waits for the recalibration.

She draws out the book she'd tucked between ribs and elbow, gestures with it, then giving the porch swing a push, she says Move over, I'll be back in a jiffy, and goes inside.

Through the screened door, from the dimly lit hall on her way to the kitchen, she shouts.

— Him. Hemingway. At the Ritz bar, I think it will be. He'll have somehow gotten into trouble, I think. Caught going around with a pistol or something. War correspondents aren't supposed to be armed, so that's just the thing he'll go for.

She comes back to the porch, the bottle of cognac in one hand, two glasses and a dog biscuit pinched between three fingers in the other.

— Hey, I said move over, she repeats. Calls Dash to jump up beside her, drags her foot to steady the swing's yaw.

Once the swing has stopped its gyrations, I pick up the thread of the story.

— Hemingway will be banned from filing stories for a week or two. Out of pure boredom, he'll turn to writing bad poetry. He'll see you at the bar, slide a chair out with his foot, give you that look, a hard stare that wants to be sure of you but the lift of one eyebrow gives it away, all his insecurities.

— Yes! He'll have just written the awfulest poem ever on a napkin. He'll read it out loud and I'll try not to be embarrassed for him, won't tell him he should stick to writing novels.

— He'll offer the napkin to you but only after signing it.

— He'll ask me to blot my lipstick on it.

— Then he'll say, On second thought, honey, I'm gonna keep that. It'll be the title poem in my anthology. I'll name it after you.

We blurt out at the same time:

— What did you say your name was, sweetheart?

A burst of laughter, we throw back our heads—a single spontaneous joy that sets the swing rocking. She rests her head on my shoulder. I start to move away, twitch her off me, Don't touch! But I take a breath and ease my head toward hers.

— Then what? she asks.

— Oh I don't know. That's enough. At least leave a little something you can write to me about.

TWENTY-NINE

IT'S BEEN A LONG DAY. Gilly is still here. We've moved to the other side of the porch, following the shade. She sits on the top step, leaning against the porch post. I've claimed the hammock. Its ropes have laid down a crosshatching of shadows across Dash, who is sprawled under me.

— No, seriously, how do I get to Paris? she asks. I don't even know if I'll get to North Africa. I may be stuck in England handing out doughnuts from clubmobiles or something boring. So how am I going to wind up in Paris?

— You'll be in North Africa when our boys beat Rommel. Then on to the Continent, the beginning of the end. Paris will be liberated. You'll ride into the city on a Jeep. The French will line the streets waving little American flags.

— Now how do you suppose they're going to have American flags handy?

— Oh, you know us. We'll have shipped over a big supply in advance, ready to give away. It will look good for the newsreels.

—Then what.

— Don't tell it all now, I say. Never mind all the talk about a quick victory; write and tell me what really happens over these next two years. At the very least, that's how long it'll take us to liberate France.

I see a look pass across her face, a question, or a statement, both: By then your box number at the post office will have been given to someone else. I will miss your funeral. Who will be there to mourn?

She recovers herself. Thank goodness. Maudlin, I do not need.

— I'll be working at American Red Cross headquarters in Paris, she says. It'll be the coldest winter ever. It'll be cold here on the Cape, too. You'll have run through all the bottles of Rémy Martin you've been hoarding since the Germans confiscated everything they could lay their hands on.

— Give me that bottle, I say.

She just laughs and pours herself a generous three fingers.

— You'll be walking past a little street just off the Rue de Rivoli, near Les Halles, I continue. You'll have just been awarded the Bronze Star in the Place du Louvre, where you have insisted that the ceremony will, at the very least, include wounded soldiers, who, you say, are more deserving.

The idea appears to have sobered her. For once, she's quiet.

— You'll be startled to see a well-dressed woman, thin and shivering. The sleeve of her fur coat grazes the rim of a trash barrel. She finds the end of a baguette and slips it in her pocket like it's a gold cigarette case, only ten times more valuable.

— I'll look away so as not to embarrass her. For that matter, I'll be starving, too.

— Don't be so dramatic, I say. No, you'll have enough to eat. You'll be warm. Or warm enough. Most likely, you'll be in love.

— Yes! Oh definitely! And you'll be the first to know. Well, the second. He'll be the first. One thing's for sure. I don't want to go hungry. Here's how it'll be. Say I'm missing a good old Thanksgiving dinner, Tranquil House style, and my beau says he can't imagine coming up with a turkey, but he'll try.

— Yes. Go on.

— And one night I come home dog-tired. I have a flat, no, a garret, five flights up. By the time I get to the second landing, I hear a terrible racket, it sounds like it's coming from my place. I open the door. It's dark inside. I raise my satchel over my head, ready to bash whoever it is. The room's a wreck, chairs are overturned. Am I keeping you in suspense?

I roll my eyes, but then, relenting, I nod.

— Okay. So what's he done, my beau? Or maybe by now he's my fiancé. I'd say yes to anyone who'd try to find a turkey for me in postwar Paris. So I see through the gloom, the noise is coming from under the deal table. I get up my nerve to look under there. And what's lover boy done? He's gone and tied two live geese to the table legs. And now I'm thinking, I'm no Maud, I'm not wringing their necks—

— All right, I've heard enough. Didn't you promise me something?

— Oh you're no fun, she says. Is she, Dash.

She goes inside. I am not to interfere. She's cooking dinner for me, a surprise, she says. As though I don't know what my own clam chowder smells like: the rich salty clams, made richer by golden butter flecking the heavy cream, thinned down with just enough milk.

She will claim her mother, that black-haired Maud, taught her the recipe. That may be so. But who was it who taught Maud how to make New England chowder? None of that broth-based gruel, not much better than ditchwater, that passes for clam chowder down at Hatteras. Who would have taught her to remove each quahog immediately, as soon as its shell steamed open? When to add the thyme?

And of course, how to make sure the chowder doesn't even so much as begin to bubble, lest the milk curdle and spoil the whole pot? The same person who taught me.

If it's halfway edible, then Gil shall have the credit. I'm prepared to go to bed hungry.

THIRTY

WE DON'T GO TO BED HUNGRY. And I must have had too much cognac, for I've invited Gilly to stay overnight. We've moved to the
garden, where the pale blue orbs of the hydrangeas glow like a con-
stellation of moons. Who knows, maybe this is where we'll sleep. Or
shall we stay up all night talking? She hasn't stopped for five minutes,
other than to slurp her chowder. Like someone I know. And like
someone else I know, she'll be asleep before long.

— I can't get that image out of my mind, she says. The black star,
passed through so many hands. And now you've made up that story
about me. Getting a Bronze Star.

Her Southern elisions, more so than the softness of her voice,
make me lean forward in my chair. I'm in the mood for stories.

— How do you know I made it up? I ask.

Even in the moonlight, I can see her roll her eyes. Or perhaps the
rich cream of the chowder is making her blink back sleep.

— Stop, she says.

— Why? Say you're in Sicily, working in a canteen, organizing
entertainment for the troops, and an explosion knocks you off your
feet. Broken leg, your one-way ticket to the States. But the Brits, suppose they have this new method of casting. You'll pitch a fit, and next

thing, you're everyone's hero, a metal cleat on the bottom of your cast, which will have so many signatures it will be more black than white, you clumping around with a crutch under one arm, handing out cigarettes with the other. I'd say that's worthy of a Bronze Star.

— Didn't you hear me, I said stop. No such thing's going to happen. Besides, the only star I ever wanted was in first grade.

She begins telling me of her own fragile star, such thin gold foil, weighted with memory. A gold star for perfect attendance, withheld.

No sooner than she begins to speak, I've formed my opinion on the matter: I hope that teacher of yours will arrive at the Pearly Gates just a few minutes tardy.

Truly, though, I hardly know what to say about someone who would not give a six-year-old child the thing she had, after all, earned. Can't imagine anyone quibbling over whether she arrived late, left early, or was altogether absent on the day of her father's funeral. But then, Gil would have given her a gold star for perfect *inattendance* at his funeral. Of all people, he would have wanted Gilly, this child he named after himself, not to mourn.

So it may have happened that the school bell had rung more than an hour before, but there little Gilly stands, atop a stool at the notions counter in the milliner's shop, a block from her family's inn on Roanoke Island. When her aunt isn't looking, she slides down, leaving behind a little black hat not much bigger than a saucer, and the sooty little pile of adornments they'd tried to interest her in: black netting, jet beads, satin ribbon, a shiny black feather, her aunt leering, their noses inches apart, twitching the feather and saying Just the thing. You love anything to do with birds, don't you? Just like your dad.

Bad children get black lumps of coal in their stockings, Gilly thinks. Good children get glittery foil stars.

She slips out the door and crosses the street to the school. She notices the flag is only halfway up the mast and thinks, Evan must have been lazy this morning, it's his turn to raise it, but it will be my turn, finally, to dust the erasers when the last bell rings this afternoon.

She stands on her toes to reach the brass doorknob, which she must use both hands to twist. Locked out! But then it opens and she tumbles into the vestibule and then another doorknob and with a shove she's in her classroom, all the children seated. She stops and announces: Gilly Lodge present, Miss Meekins, I'm here, just a little tardy, and then walks to her desk.

She can hear the restless stir of her classmates' voices, like the sound of the tide rising in the marsh when it lisps through the salt hay.

Miss Meekins tells her she must go home, but she sits and holds tight to the scarred edge of her desk and stares past the teacher at the magical shapes swimming across the blackboard, their bellies full of secret messages swallowed whole, the *W* and the *O* especially beloved, and of course, the *G* and the *L*, all the letters, more than she can count on two hands and two feet, caught in the net made by the teacher's lovely straight lines chalking across the board.

Inside a book, when the letters swim together in a school, they spawn words, her father says, and in the way that puppy drum and flounder and mackerel each have their own patterns, fin set here, eye just there, she recognizes certain words by their shapes. First, little words, *the* and *and*, flash by like minnows. Of course her names, *Gilly* and *Winstead* and *Lodge*, and his, *Papa*, come floating up whole out of the massy squiggles black as a skate's purse. Bigger words lurk, basking sharks crowding the little ones on the page, and these must be sounded out. *Orange* looks like itself, bright and round and succulent, the *G* soft and tangy. *G-U-E-S-S* is such a surprise, a square package trailing ribbons, with a great big smile called *U*, it brings on gleeful laughter and a clapping of hands. *Glitter,* another hard-*G* word, sparkles in her mind like the gold star, pointy bright. Whenever Miss Meekins asks for a word that begins with *CH*, she sings out, *Chicamacomico*!

Her father covers her hand with his and together they trace letters in the sand, or their fingers swim words through the water as they lean over the gunnel, his oar holding them steady in the current. *Kingfisher*, they shout, scripting the air with his spyglass. *Egret*, scrawled in the sand with an anchor's rusted fluke.

There is a night when he waits for her to think of a word, his hand ready to guide her pointed finger across the cold windowpane papered white with ice crystals. She sings out four crisp new letters: *S-W-A-N*! In the spangled glass he sees his reflection and none other's gleaming, and how is she to know of the swan hovering over a faraway bed or the one who sleeps there still. He drops her hand and turns away, forgetting to tuck her in.

After the teacher leaves the room, Gilly writes with her finger on the desk, and her fingertip jumps over and butts against the other letters filleted into the wood decades ago by some now dead boy's knife, as she spells *Papa, Papa, Papa*.

When the hotel porter arrives, he carries her screaming from the classroom, down the street, back home to the Tranquil House Inn.

THIRTY-ONE

WHAT MUST IT BE LIKE FOR THEM, I think, how the Lodges are always drawing attention to themselves? They have a baby grand, the only piano within fifty miles, save for the few slightly out-of-tune uprights that sit waiting to play for Sunday's congregation. They live at Tranquil House, the family's inn, except in summer, when they move across the street to a gabled house with not one but two parlors: one to receive visitors, the privileged few, and one for Maud and her four daughters, Gil forever gone, barefoot and hatless, over to Bodie Island or maybe further south, across the inlet, to Pea Island and on down to Hatteras. Those oldest girls, Mary Maud and Sophie and Natalie, had their portraits made in Boston. In their oval gilt frames they hang like royalty on the flocked walls of the main parlor at Tranquil House.

Yet their mother is not from this proud little metropolis of Manteo, the county seat, where they've only recently passed a law against spitting tobacco on the courtroom floor but have yet to outlaw cows roaming the streets, which, after the least rain shower, are a sea of churned-up mud, until the Town Fathers finally see fit to send a crew to oyster them.

Maud is from Chicamacomico down the Banks, from the island where *Kinnakeeters! Yaupon Eaters!* live, or at least that's what the Roanoke Islanders chant when Hatteras Islanders come to town. Chicamacomico north and south, Kinnakeet, the Cape, Trent, Hatteras, one village is indistinguishable from another to those who live just one island to the northwest. As far as people on Roanoke Island are concerned, the only time you see those "Hatt'rsmen" is when they're hauled in by the sheriff on court days. No need to drag them in sooner, a waste of a good jail cell, Hatteras being prison enough to hold them until the judge comes to town.

And Gilead Lodge, their father, a divorced (or was he) Yankee carpetbagger who built his new Hotel Roanoke a stone's throw from Asa Evans's Tranquil House just to run him out of business, and when he couldn't, that Yankee sold his own hotel at a premium and bought the inn at a steal, so they say.

For years beyond counting, Maud, both lord and lady of the inn, would rise tiredly and say, Well I guess I best go kill a chicken, in case Mr. Lodge comes home tonight—as though ten o'clock were a proper time to be chasing a tough old bird around the pitch-black yard, her lantern light flaring wildly if there was no moon, leaving her guests to wonder if this Mr. Lodge, whom they had yet to meet, would return from his Bodie Island camp before their visit ended. The smell of scalded feathers rose up the stairs, uneasy on the landings, peckish at the guestroom doors.

At some point her neighbors would pass this story up and down Water Street, across porch railings twined with morning glories and down along white picket fences pricked with salt roses or billowed with the fat blue heads of hydrangeas, saying, He could wring his own chicken's neck, you wouldn't catch me waiting up for him, much less waiting on him.

If it wasn't too late in the evening, they would discuss all over again whether that circuit-riding judge with the last name of Starbuck, a proper Nantucket name, you know, whether that transplanted

Yankee judge who was probably a friend of his from up at Cape Cod, you know how they stick together, whether the divorce he granted was maybe legal, maybe not, maybe all these years he had himself two wives, one young, one old.

— Well, he were a handsome thing when he first come here, if you like them dark and broody.

They all rock, pushing off the railings where the morning glories are shut tight, or holding onto the ropes of their porch swings as they stir the scented air, heel-toeing the gray floorboards on nights when there is no breeze and it's humid enough for fish to walk on land.

— Weren't he though?

Perhaps that's what the women say as they sit lined up on their porches, thinking their children are asleep. Instead, the little ones crouch by the windows, breathing in the grown-ups' stories, hot and humid, until they fall in a sticky dreaming heap.

What must it have been like for Maud, then, her Mr. Lodge always off with his dog and his gentlemen and his ducks, at last come home, even now, not to stay for long. Laid out in the guest parlor of the uppity white house they call "over home," across from the inn, soon enough, the last clod of earth falls heavy on his fine new mahogany abode, and he lies with his head pointing east, ready to face the rising sun on Judgment Day. What will last in memory? The epitaph she had carved into soft, white Carrera marble? The neighbors' gossip, pulled and champed at like salt taffy? Or these, my hoard of stories?

What they don't know or say, I will recall, for I know him better than any, better than even she, who had him last and longest.

THIRTY-TWO

EVERYONE, GILLY SAID, OR MIGHT HAVE SAID, was whispering. Unless her mother and sisters passed by. Then they all hushed. In the field where the stones grow, it was cold. There were no trees to block the wind. But they were going to plant a new tree, and it would make shade, and when the wind blew, the shadows would lie down on the ground and the wind would show itself, clutching handfuls of grass in its shadow branches.

All the grown-ups stood around a deep hole next to a pile of dirt. Gilly slipped her hand out of her sister Mary Maud's and eeled her way to the edge. Her father wasn't there, but nearly all his friends were, it seemed, and a lot of others who weren't. She reached up and tugged on Tucker Daniels's suspender, but he moved away.

Tucker, Screenwire, Judge Starbuck, Mercy Tillett, Cap'n Baum, and Lish Meekins put straps under a wooden box and planted it down in the hole so the wood would grow into a new tree. The box was made of a mahogany tree. She thought trees grew from nuts or cones or seeds, not boards or boxes. Everyone said in their whispery voices that it was expensive, came in on the *Trenton*, pine weren't good enough, typical extravagance, Yankee airs.

She would ask Papa to show her a mahogany tree so she wouldn't have to wait for it to grow out of the ground to see the shape of its leaves and the way the bark grew and how the branches spread, although this mahogany tree, growing from boards, had a head start over a little nut in its shell and so would probably grow pretty fast. She would come and water the box every day and when the tree grew, she would ask Papa to toss up a rope and hang a burlap sack from its branch to make a swing.

Once the graveside service was over, the mourners would have mingled around the table in the inn's dining room, sampling from the innumerable dishes prepared under Mrs. Lodge's dogged instruction. The ladies who talked about him on their porches would be there, along with their husbands, the leaders of town and county. There, too, were the men who loved him, keepers and surfmen from all seven life-saving stations, the fishermen and the lightkeepers and the hunters, who did not care if his house had two parlors or whether the rumors were true that he'd built an exact replica of his other wife's house back north, up at Cape Cod.

Say that Gilly squeezes between the people crowded around the dining room table that, with its extra walnut leaves in place, is big as a shad boat. She can usually walk under it if she bends slightly at the waist, but with her mother's best lace tablecloth laid, she must crawl beneath it like a seine net. She is a smart fish.

She pulls the edge of the lace cloth hard against her jawbone. Gilled, she whispers. Gilly. Now I'm a speckled trout hung up in Papa's gill net that I helped to mend. Urgggh. She flops over.

During her often-lauded imitation of a dying-fish gasp, she smells something good. Rhubarb pie, her father's favorite and therefore hers. She crawls out long enough to slip a piece under the table, where she eats it with her fingers, wiping them on the carpet while there are plenty of guests to take the blame.

Such a feast. There is Thanksgiving food, and Christmas and Easter, Fourth of July food, birthday food, all the famous Tranquil House fare at once, sitting right above her head. She likes that Papa lets Mama take all the credit, even though they are his recipes. Mary Maud and Sophie and Natalie say it tastes like Boston.

She lets the voices lap around her and pretends she's in Papa's shad boat, leaning against a table leg as though it were the mast. A word or a phrase will sometimes wash up but mostly what she hears is vibration, the sound of the ocean sipping and sipping at the foamy lip of a conch shell's unfathomed depths, saying *schhhhhhrrrrr*.

In the slosh of voices, Mrs. Burrus might be telling Mrs. Wescott how they had to carry that littlest one screaming out of school, and part of the story must have been how she had flung off the brand-new hat Miss Price made just for the occasion, because of course she is so young, this is her first funeral, she has never had the need of a black hat until now.

— I heard that before she stomped on it, ground it right into the dirt, they said, she really threw a tantrum, pulled the black feather out of the velvet hat band and tore it all to pieces.

— Now that I hadn't heard.

— Yes, well, what do you expect.

— I know what you're thinking. Spoiled rotten with him sixty-nine nigh on seventy when she was born. Old enough to be her grandfather.

— Or great-grandfather.

— Too old, by any measure.

— Yes, too old. Truth be told, too old for mother and daughter alike. Here, have some of Maud's sweet potato biscuits.

The women rattle on, recalling the northeaster that made up off-shore the night Gilly was born, Gil flinging out of the house after midnight, Maud sure he'd drowned on the way to Bodie Island, how he was the one who was spoiled, Maud putting up with his disappearances, his disappointments.

— Here, have another. Yes, and a pity she would feel the need to explain his absence with that morbid thought instead of coming right out with it and saying, 'The old goat is never home, what's the difference.' But to leave without saying kiss my foot to Maud who had labored for the fourth time, there's just no excuse.

The women have taken up permanent residence at one end of the table, continuing to hash over how much Gilly looks like her belated father, the poor thing, saddled with that name, whatever he could do to make her into a boy, keeping her hair chopped off and letting her run barefoot in short pants instead of dresses.

— Maud had 'Lavinia' all picked out, after her sister. But he put his foot down.

— Here, put some of these in your purse to take home. The linen napkin, too, they won't miss it, wrap the biscuits in it.

Gilly sits under the table, tasting the words, holding to her chest the orange her father had given her just the day before yesterday. Legs mill and shift, and some she recognizes: Mrs. Tillett's thick ankles, Mr. Dough's polished brogues, Marsh Daniels's waders an insult (he could have shown more respect for Mr. Lodge's passing, if not for my Turkey carpet, her mother will say). Gilly looks for, but doesn't really expect to see, her father's gumboots. He is so seldom home. Crumbs fall on the carpet, crushed underfoot. A vein of spilled Madeira bleeds down the white lace cloth. She sucks the lace and licks her lips.

She knows all about dying. When fish are shoveled onto the dock they lie still and cold, then flap when you least expect it. Eventually, their colors fade, their eyes go flat. Frog legs jump all around in the pan, just legs, no frogs. When Dash dies you dig a big hole but not as big as the one for Dave the ox, which would have been bigger if they hadn't chopped off his legs with the ax, poor Dave, and all for the sake of a smaller hole. Chickens aren't quite dead, going about headless as though they're still looking for worms, which can still wriggle even after you put the hook through them. So when they say poor child your dear papa is dead she knows he will never fit in a hole because he's far too tall, they wouldn't dare take an ax to his legs, and his eyes are too blue to go all flat. Too blue, with sparks of other blue in them.

And so she pays no attention, but when he doesn't come home for a month and more, she sails across Shallowbag Bay in the little skiff they built together. She aims for Wanchese Wharf, where she intends to put two Orange Crushes on his account before sailing on to the hunt club at Bodie Island. The tide sweeps her across the sound and up into a twist of marsh. Her skiff parts the salt creek called Maggie's Drawers, where the reedy banks press inward like two defiant knees and the wind rears back from the sulfurous stink of marsh gas. She knows which curves of the creek to hug, working her tiller to find an inch or two of deeper water, but the tide is high and swift and it thrusts her bow into a thatch of marsh, her bottom stuck fast in oozy black mud that six hours before was hard baked and scuttled with cracks, as it will be again come six hours later.

Her sail luffs and then stills. She pushes against the bank with her shove-pole but it sticks hard, nearly vaulting her out of the boat and so she sits, furious, sweaty, and fly-bitten, her head no higher than the black needlerush so that when the men come upon her, their arrival is announced by the red-winged blackbirds startled from their uncertain footholds on the slender reeds.

They haul her into the boat they had unloosed from Cap'n Charlie Pugh's slip without his say-so, seeing as how it was an emergency. Towing her skiff behind, they snake their way through Maggie's Drawers. To Gilly's delight, the men get stuck twice before making the secret turn into Broad Creek, which she agrees to show them only if they will let her go on to Bodie Island.

Trapped in their grown-up store-bought selves and therefore incapable of keeping their promises, the men do not aim the tiller south-southeast as they enter the mouth of Broad Creek and on into Pamlico Sound toward Bodie Island, but instead bear west, toward Wanchese. There at the wharf sits the Model T with "Sleep in Tranquility" stenciled in white on the door, the dangly parts of the "p" and the "q" and the "y" smeared where Dash had wagged his tail before the paint could dry.

Ordinary bird drama mixes with the shouts of a flailing child, the gulls hysterical over a stale heel of bread or a fish head. Leaving her boat at the dock, the men drive her home. The gulls settle back on the pilings.

The orange, her own ripe round word that would become a kind of bequest, will shrivel in a week or a month. It sits on her dresser like a shrunken pockmarked face, there next to the starfish still smelling of brine, a gold star she has awarded herself, until her mother makes her throw them both away.

Poor child. The class roll on November 27, 1924, shows her absent that day, when I could have told her, it was her father who was the absent one, all his livelong life.

THIRTY-THREE

GILLY SLEPT IN THE HAMMOCK THAT FIRST NIGHT. I didn't sleep at all. She's now ensconced in an upstairs bedroom, the one with the gabled eaves. She likes cubbyholes, she says. She doesn't like lumpy mattresses. Too bad, I say. What are you going to do when you have to sleep in a tent out in the desert, I ask her. She says I just made that up, she's going to be in London, working in a Red Cross clubmobile.

She's pilfered a few of Gil's shirts and one of his hats. The shirts I don't mind. The hat I do. And Dash. I mind Dash. At the very least, he could sleep in my room on the nights I manage to sleep. But no, he climbs the steps each night without so much as a backward glance.

She says she wants to talk about something else, she's tired of her childhood. I say, that's a shame, since you're still in it. But I know what she means. She's ready to hear more about Gil's life here, which means my life. At least she's stopped going on about that list of hers, how rude I was to tear it up, and how many of the questions still haven't been answered.

And how many of them, in fact, will I answer? The white spaces between the lines, what do they leave unsaid?

THIRTY-FOUR

IT WASN'T LONG AFTER GIL RETURNED from his 1866 trip to Cape Hatteras that I proposed to him. Well, not precisely. He did leave me some dignity, although there wasn't much you could do about the fact that he was seventeen and I was twenty-five. But I was the one who summed up his life at that point—still aimless—and laid out a path for him that just happened to include me and the steady government pay of a surfman at the Chatham Beach Life-Saving Station.

The money didn't matter to me. But since he said he wanted to support me, instead of living off my inheritance, the service seemed a good match. Men sought work at the station in spite of the danger and the boredom. The day-to-day extremes had a rhythm that fit his habits, left him room for his birds and fish. And, I thought, for me.

It wasn't until after he was appointed keeper of the station that we were married. Those five years between proposal and wedding might have been awkward if I'd listened to what I knew was whispered or said outright. Instead I ignored the talk and set about doing what both our fathers had asked of me when Gil was a boy, to be his tutor. But who taught?

What I learned was how to tell, when blindfolded by his hands, the difference between snow geese and Canadas, by the whistling of their wings. I took as my primer his knowledge of the flats, the tidal creeks, the currents. I took his text on cirrus by day, comet trail by night. He schooled me in all the ways of knowing.

My teacher wore no tie. His black hair looked like the tide had run through it and dried, leaving a fine tracing of salt along his hairline, silty across the tops of his brows. Other times, his hair stood up not of its own volition or at the whim of any tide, but due to his habit of tugging at its roots, fist clenched. Sticky with salt air or fish scales, it tended to stay, the scales iridescent as fly wings. I learned to search out the faint briny smell of it, me with my carefully dried rose petals and the buds of beach plums, loving his elemental odor of quartz and iodine. He smelled alive.

He taught me to watch, but how was he to know what I observed? The birds he loved, yes, but only because in them I saw him. His movements were compact, summoning power, like a bird gathering itself before flight, every feather in service to the sky. Whether sitting on the sea or clutching the rim of its nest, a bird's whole being is anti-earth, anti-gravity, all air. Like a bird, he was a creature of movement and if there was joy in it, it was the joy of instinct, no need to express it outright. Feeling was sufficient.

Him I lectured on Renaissance paintings and Greek myths, Roman sculpture and the Romantic poets, so that he fell in love with me and with Leda and her long-necked swan, Zeus transformed, together begetting the beautiful Helen in a white rush, who then comes tapping her way out of a translucent eggshell, her face destined to beguile fleet upon fleet of ships.

He would make me recite the poems Ben once loved, even though he knew them as well as I. As the stanzas hypnotized with their own intrinsic rhythm, he would hold a fingertip enthralled at the twisted blue vein pulsing at my temple, where it surfaced and then submerged like an embroidered knot of silk. I imagined he could count the echoed heartbeats held there beneath alabaster skin.

On the day there were three heartbeats pulsing, mine and two others, we married.

THIRTY-FIVE

THEIR WEDDING WAS MORE INTERESTING THAN MINE. I read about it in the *Chatham Monitor*. But first I heard about it at our local stationer's, where he'd ordered their engraved invitations.

Captain and Mrs. Griffin O'Neal
Request the honor of your presence
At the marriage of their daughter
Anna Maud O'Neal
to
Gilead Winstead Lodge
Thursday, February 1, 1900
Two o'clock p.m.
At the home of the bride
Rodanthe, North Carolina

I know why he needed an engraver, none to be had on that forsaken island where a printing press would have been as strange as a steam locomotive. But who can say why he would send the wedding announcement to the Chatham newspaper for anyone with five cents and a pair of spectacles to hash over. After all, minutes after Dunn

Stationers received the order, all Chatham knew about it, and all Chatham made sure I knew about it, too. The newspaper could have saved its ink.

Perhaps I'll give Miss Gillian the invitation. Her mother doesn't seem especially sentimental, so If she's to have any memento of her mother and father's wedding it will be mine to give. I've kept it tucked in the frame of his shaving mirror, or sometimes propped on my nightstand, or in a crystal placeholder set between their two Spode plates, where the two of them, Mr. Lodge and Mrs. Lodge the Second, occasionally keep me company.

Their daughter insists that today we go for a walk. At first I say no, but she's grabbed my old straw hat hanging on a peg by the door and stands there waiting. It'll be good to go on a ramble along the cliff.

Gilly says she loves the salt roses, their blowsy red petals vivid against the blue of Chatham Harbor. She has yet to see them at their best, when a southwest wind rolls the fog through them, the petals blown free from their fringed yellow centers so that the gray skies seem to be raining red.

For many years I cursed those rugosas. Too many times my hands have sprinkled their furrowed leaves with drops of blood. I would tear them out by their roots and fling them over the cliff no sooner than Gil would put them in the ground. Who's to say what should be in the cradle and what in the grave.

Once on a windy day, the roses with their vicious thorns blew back on an updraft, scratching my face in neat, close rows, my skin fallow ground for their crop of thorns. That evening, Gil said nothing. The next morning, a new hedge of salt roses sat, their smug petals an insult, the door at the end of the hall locked once more, a new hiding place for the key.

Now that I think of it, that was one of the times he went south.

As we walk along the cliff's edge, a kingfisher flies up and startles me. Gilly thinks I've stumbled on the path brittle with oyster shells. I let her hold my elbow for a few steps. I do not tell her the bird's wingbeats, its distinctive rattled cry, simply shocked me. I've become accustomed to my birds, so still and quiet in my parlor, it couldn't have startled me more if a lamp had flapped its fringed shade and cawed like any black crow.

We sit on the bench Gil made for me out of scrimshawed whalebone. I don't feel much like talking about that one's wedding, or mine. I would like to ask Gilly a few questions myself, but we sit quietly, each lost in our own imaginings of the ebb and flow of two marriages that finally tossed Gilly and me here together on the shore.

Later I may feel like telling her about our fine citizens, how they huddled over their invitations filched from the engraver's trash barrel. Perhaps we'll discuss whether it ever occurred to them to wonder why Gil and his southern belle would be married on a Thursday, at home. Or perhaps not. This subject might best be left unsaid.

After all, the announcement left out a few choice facts, such as how he, a man exactly three times her age—if I am correct that seventeen times three equals fifty-one—was marrying a girl who had turned him down flat even before her aunts had confirmed he was still married. The announcement forgot to say how he waited for a Nantucket man who had relocated south to make the judicial circuit, how his cronies from Hatteras filled the jury box, how he got his divorce only six months after he'd left me here in Chatham, a year and a half sooner than the North Carolina law allows, three and a half years sooner than Massachusetts.

I had fetched him home once. Appeal the court's decision? I'd have sooner appealed to Lucifer to get me into Heaven, with just as much success.

Does that make Gilly and her three sisters illegitimate? I could toss that idea out to her, but she's had enough surprises on this trip. What do legal niceties matter when it comes to children, anyway. They are incontrovertible in their suchness. What do salmon care about the date of their offsprings' spawning, and would a pair of cardinals shame their hatchlings for the simple fact of being born? They wish them well in the world, whatever path life's journey may take, whoever else helps them on their way. No, this I will not call to her attention, and I'll hope she doesn't think to ask.

What I do mention is that the little news item in the *Monitor* forgot to inform our local populace how even after our divorce she still turned Gil down, threw his ring into his bait bucket and dared him to fish it out. How she paraded a boy her own age up and down the Banks until Gil, her one and only hope of getting off the island, was finally persuaded to give up his dream of living, barefoot and bareheaded, off the land and sea.

If he were going to move across the Pamlico to Roanoke Island and the marginally more civilized county seat of Manteo, he might as well have stayed in Chatham.

Take me off this sand bank, she demanded, and move us to town. You built a hotel on the beach at Cape Cod for *her* to run? I want a hotel on Roanoke Island. Our children are going to be born in Manteo.

Those were her terms. He accepted them, even if the church didn't. Apparently neither did her parents, the happy couple banished to the porch, their vows spirited away by the wind.

The announcement he sent to our newspaper left out these little facts, but then, he was ever light on words.

THIRTY-SIX

— WAIT. STOP, Gilly says. Go back.

She startles me. Have I been speaking, after all? She's jumped up off the bench and is standing in front of me, her hands on her hips.

— What in the world must have been going on in my mother's mind? she asks.

— Well, maybe you should have asked her that before you came all the way up here. That would have been a good start. Likely a good finish as well. You probably would never have had the nerve to come to Chatham after that. Nevertheless, I've actually given that quite a bit of thought. There are times when I enjoy a little dalliance inside the skull of Miss Anna Maud. Would you like to join me? I ask. I'll oblige and take you there.

I think she may actually be getting ready to pout. But she surprises me and takes the challenge.

— Okay, go ahead. No. Wait. Let me try.

What does she think this is, a game? This is my story. I am the one who has the final say about it. She can't appropriate my life. It's already been stolen once. By her mother. And now she thinks she can step right up and take it again.

— No. I'll tell you exactly what your mother would have said. You supply a name or two. Who's her best friend? Garnet, wasn't that her name? What was her horse called?

Now she really is pouting.

— Don't be a bore, I say. And where did that pout come from? Your father did a fine job of pouting in his mind, but he never let it make it to his lips. Must be a trait of hers, that Maud. Yes, hold that look. It will give me something to work with when I tell you what your mother was up to.

— No, really, let me try.

— You act as if I'm making this up. I know what I know.

— I don't care. She's my mother. And I'm going to tell you what she would have been thinking about this whole thing.

I say nothing.

She sits back down.

— Garnet. Garnet Farrow, she says. And Gracie. Her Banker pony's name was Gracie.

— All right, then.

I begin.

THIRTY-SEVEN

BY THE TIME WE GET A NEWSPAPER DOWN HERE, the news is so old it stinks like week-old fish. Gossip, it stinks, too, especially if it's about you, but somehow that gets here a whole lot faster. The sun didn't hardly have time to set before word of the five-line legal announcement reached Chicamacomico. A wife? There's a wife? How can there be a wife when I have an engagement ring on my left hand. I actually looked to see if I'd imagined it.

It was Garnet Farrow who told me and if Garnet knew, all of Dare County knew. There was no better peddler of gossip on the entire run of the Banks. People living back of the beach in Nags Head Woods or Kitty Hawk Village, or up north past Duck and on up to Whales Head, even all the way across Croatan Sound to Mashoes on the mainland, they might not know me. But they'd sure know as how somebody named Maud O'Neal over to Chicamacomico was engaged to a married man.

Worse, if Garnet knew, then my father did, too. He's the kind that'll tip his cap at any soul he meets, will risk his life to dredge you up out of the ocean, will sit you down at his table, he'll even let you sleep in his bed. But you lie to him just once, you may as well be a ghost because he will look straight through you. Well not even a ghost, since any normal person wouldn't stay in a room with one. But he'd go right on about his business, clean his pipe then fill it, cross the room for a match, light it, puffing on the stem with that pff pff pff sound til the tobacco in the bowl catches fire, the aroma of ripe cherries grabbing you by the nose, and if you were between him and his chair, he'd pay no mind whatsoever, keep right on walking, so's even a ghost would feel the need to move out of his way.

So here I go telling it like it were some ordinary thing, like news that one of the neighbors just died from eating chocolate after oysters, which ever since Tull Meekins keeled over at the dinner table, everybody knows is a deadly combination. But I can't deny, it fairly swamped me. It was all I could do to keep myself afloat in front of Garnet.

Now my mother, she's a different story. She will, as the saying goes, make a purse out of a sow's ear. I did my best imitation of her. I put my thumbs inside my waistband, reared back, threw my bosom out as far as it would go, which if I do say so myself, was a considerable distance, and replied to Garnet, "Well of course. He's a man of the world. He had another life. But. He chose me." I turned, head high, walked off the porch of Mr. Mac's store where gossip is stocked on the shelves right alongside five-pound bags of flour, mounted Gracie, and left at a slow trot. It nearly knocked my teeth out of my head. I was so mad I would've spit them all out like a chaw of stale tobacco.

I reined Gracie into a walk, which bareback on a Banker pony in the deep sand is more like a hard plod. But as soon as we were out of sight and down on the flats, I kicked her twice in the ribs and gave her her head, like I could outrun the fury, outrun it or trample it down. But it rode on my back, the fury did, until its weight slowed us to a walk, then to a standstill. I slipped sideways off Gracie and let the waves wash around me. Water's always been a healing thing.

Why the news of a wife surprised anyone, and especially my family, I don't know. There was plenty enough talk about that Yankee woman who came and took him away in the winter of '93, or guess you'd say '94 since it was January, right around Epiphany, what we call Old Christmas. I remember because I turned twelve and got my first monthlies and had to stay home, missed seeing the men blundering around under an old cowhide dressed up like Old Buck, poking people with their horns like that's what's needed to stir up a fistfight when who needs an excuse. Anyway, the talk only lasted about a year, which around here is nothing. When he came back the next fall, all nonchalant, that's a French word for don't pay it no mind, I like the sound of it, he was all nonchalant like he left here under his own steam instead of trailing in her wake like a gilled fish on a stringer.

The wife up there made sure everyone knew she was Mrs. Lodge, but with her being older than him, and so Yankee-like in her ways, he'd been around here long enough so's he seemed more like one of us than anything attached to her.

And I mean to keep it that way.

THIRTY-EIGHT

— So. How DID I DO? I ask Gilly.

— Is that really what happened? Then I'll have to thank you for that. You've saved me from having to ask my mother when I get home. How embarrassing.

— I'm the one he left. You don't say one word to me about embarrassing.

She raises an eyebrow but I will not give ground.

— Anyway, you pretty well pegged my mother. And my grandparents. That was actually a fair likeness of them.

While I've been talking, she's sagged down on the sand in front of me and practically dug her way to China. She's taken it well, considering how she flew out of my house that first day and ran all the way to the Mattaquason, where she did or did not lock herself in her room for days. And how would it be my fault, all that upset? I'm not the one who sent her here unarmed with even the most basic of facts, namely, me. At any rate, she seems to be settling into reality. I'll have to give her that.

— All right, let's go, I say. You must be tired. Look at that hole.

She moves aside, and Dash plops himself into the cool spot she's made in the sand.

— No, don't stop. Now what.

A cold day, then, in February, there at Chicamacomico or Rodanthe or whatever that place is called, the house with its back to the sea now standing a little more upright than when I first saw it, stiffened with a coat of paint and a room or two added on, a twist of gingerbread in an eave. The wind, as ever, is out of the northeast, but the porch is sheltered in the southwest ell of the house so that Maud O'Neal's dress, which still bears the wrinkles of four days' hard travel, coming south on the train, the steamer, the mail boat, then lightered to shore on a skiff, the white wedding gown that had traveled all the way from Boston now barely moves except for the tremor of a young girl's longing or is it reluctance, such that it makes the hem of her organza gown cover and uncover the toes of her satin slippers. Perhaps it was only the wind toying with her veil, swirling and then snagging it on the splintered floorboards of the porch where, five years earlier, she'd sat like an angel, waist-deep in a cloud of white feathers.

Two hundred invitations fresh off Mr. Dunn's platen press were hand delivered, if it can be believed there were two hundred people to populate such a place, but then where would they go, one island remote as the next, and all of them kin. But there is room enough for all in attendance there on the porch, not much bigger than a good-sized pantry but at least forty degrees colder. The bride and groom, of course the preacher, and the bride's father, exchanging plumes of breath like kisses or curses made visible, while the bride's mother has stayed inside. Too proud or too ashamed, amounting to the same, she peers from behind the curtain just in time to read the preacher's lips at the relevant part, *I now pronounce you.*

My wedding was also a stone's throw from the sea. It was even more sparsely attended. I did not wear white.

THIRTY-NINE

*WHEN I STEPPED THROUGH THE SHANTY DOOR, Gil and the captain of
the Nell stood waiting, the groom with a salt rose in his* buttonhole,
the captain holding a sea-swollen Bible. The ocean was our altar.
Our children were the only attendants, asleep in the cradle of my
womb.

I couldn't say how Gil looked, for here was a sight so longed for
that it seemed a dream, and like a dream, its impress on the mind is
indelible, yet the details hover just out of reach. What I do recall is
that he took a step backward. There are days when I think it was an
omen, that he was leaving before we had even arrived at our vows.
There are other days, when I am kind to myself, that I think he stood
back to take in the sight of me, there in my bridal gown, on the precipice of both marriage and motherhood.

No, the dress was not white, but skeins of gray silk overlaying a
gray satin sheath. It had taken nearly five years to tat the gown. Since
I never expected to wear it, I was in no hurry. In the evenings when
he was mounting his birds, on foggy days when he tied cork floats
along a length of net, all the interminable days of life-saving patrols
or a run of bluefish in spring or the first flush of birds in the fall, I
had ample time.

I can't say when the idea came to tie myself all tight-netted in lace. Tatting an entire dress, with its thousands and thousands of knots, was an unimaginable task.

When I first took up the shuttle, the whalebone needle darting through my fingers like a fish flirting with a morsel of bait, a wedding dress was the last thing on my mind. I was only seeking a way to emulate—or perhaps irritate—Gil. How would he like it if, hour upon hour, I sat silent, working away on dead things, when there was a living being sitting there beside him aching for attention? Oddly, it wasn't long before a bit of lace dangling from its chain of tiny knots became a kind of resurrection. What if, like Gil, I could capture the living essence of a bird?

Where he would strip a sanderling of its cloak of feathers and coax it onto a wooden form, I wanted to dress my bird, adding a new layer of subterfuge to nature's own camouflage. I could claim its soul twice over.

I imagined Gil dismissing my work. Like tatting a skullcap on an actual skull, what's the point, he might have said. But even my earliest efforts he made note of, if not effusively. Takes skill, he said, and those two words I could live on for years.

Before I was ready to try shorebirds, I had to reteach myself how to tat, making the fingers of one hand do the work of a loom, the other fingers shuttling in and out. First I started with quahogs, laying spiraled chains of silk along the shell's ribbed curves. They ended up looking like lumps of dough, so next I experimented with fish, making knots half the size of caviar. I spun each vertebra, fin ray, and rib, so that the sea trout wore two skeletons, one lace, one bone.

My first try with a bird was modest, a wren that had dashed itself against the windowpane. Formulating a mixture of lime, salt, and alum to preserve my specimens, I went on to larger birds filched from Gil's game bag. Weaving the graceful, drooping plumes of an egret, I starched the lace feathers so they would hold their shape as I dressed the bird in its new raiment of knotted string. I did not think of myself as a taxidermist but rather a couturier.

A bird can be the drabbest creature on earth and yet the most elaborately clothed. Each quill in itself is perfection. When laid feather on feather across a plump breast, the pattern is exquisite. An outstretched wing, fanning air, reveals the subtlest coloration, absolute artistry. The detail is minute. How to embellish what cannot be improved upon? I began experimenting with colored threads, the finest silk, my lace an iridescence.

No longer. The birds on the mantel sag down, a wing bone or beak protruding from the faded threads. The fish that swam in white schools on the shelf, they now lie exhausted amid pooling yellow skirts of lace, sad in their shapeless spiny heaps. They smell faintly of brine.

As for the gown, it's still lovely. Or it was. The last time I tried it on, I could tell the top of my head would no longer fit just beneath Gil's chin. Old age shortens both height and memory. For years, the gown lived on a dress form by our bed, our wedding portrait looking over its shoulder. Today, wrapped in tissue, it lies folded in a trunk in the rafters of the boathouse. Or perhaps I threw it on the pile of gillnets spilling out of the net shed.

Five years of our lives are there, bound up in gray silk. Into the design I poured all ways of keeping Gil close, or if not close, then constant, as the night sky is constant, its rotation predetermined, like the circling of a hawk with its promise to return, if not now, then surely next season. And so knotted tight, cinching the waist of my wedding gown, is Orion on the hunt, the Pleiades forming the dress's train. Down one side, an osprey in flight shakes water droplets from his wings. Down the other, he kicks higher, a fish's tail now flapping deep in his belly. At the throat, I knotted the geometric intention of a spider backing and winding around the spotted wings of a moth. Circling each elbow, silken chains follow the endless inward curve of a moon snail blanketed by waves.

Of course, there are swans. Feathering down along the gown's sleeves are the necks of a cob and a pen, their slender beaks tapering to a point at my fingertips. Leda and her swan, their children hatched from eggs, these stories I told in twists and knots and rings. I tatted our lives together, laying the picots and the double-hitched lark's heads and the Josephine knots down like a winged shadow.

The night I finished knotting the many scenes together and first swam up into the gown's fantastical net, I stood before the pier glass and beheld silk alchemized into water. Ripples, pools, reflections, wavelets, droplets, waterfalls; a cascade of thread lapped and curled around my body like water takes hold of a hand submerged, each finger gloved in transparency.

On my wedding day, I flowed out of the shanty, onto the beach, and the words effervesced around us. To have, to hold, never to be parted, not even unto death. I do.

FORTY

It's a mild day, fair enough to cross over to the beach. Alone. I've told Gilly I need breathing room. She can do without me for a day. Go poke around Seaside Cemetery. The Eldredge Library. Make the trip from Chatham to Harwich to feel for yourself the lengths to which Gil went to disguise his escape in 1893, when he abandoned the poor team of horses at the Harwich station rather than boarding the train for New York directly from Chatham. Go. Explore. Anything other than staying stuck underneath me all day. Now that her Red Cross duties have been postponed for three more weeks, I need space.

Last night's storm has swept the beach clean, a wide beach, built up overnight so that it's nearly as expansive as the year when Gil first built his shanty. I ease down and rest my cheek on the sand where the beach is flat as cardboard, cool but not damp. The angle of the scarp, at eye level, becomes even more acute, the sea sheeting away to infinity. It sets me free not only to see but to feel the tilt of the earth, off-kilter, throttling through space and time.

On a day such as this, five decades ago, Gil and I lie on this beach, or its facsimile, our clothes like wet sandpaper. We shed them, gritty skin against skin an extra layer of sweet friction sharpening our pleasure, sealing it. On his back, one arm beneath me, the other outflung, he raises my head slightly, turns my face toward his, and whispers, We are not spinning smoothly, the earth is off balance, I feel an irresistible urge to leave.

I wait for, and do not hear, *and to return*. I wait for him to explain himself. He doesn't. I turn my head away.

In a minute or an hour, he says, What would life be like if the earth were at right angles to the sun. Nothing would change. Then you'd be happy.

My heart shifts in my chest as though it were a planet he had just picked up and moved, to circle a different star.

I am happy, I say.

Silence.

Except for the ocean, which has never been quiet, not ever, not even on the calmest day. Gil props himself on his elbow, looks at me, with that way he has of blotting out everything but what he puts before me. The ocean, that ocean, goes away. It's now his ocean that I see, hear, taste, could drown in.

It's why whales move, he says. The upwelling of the oceans, bringing more life to the surface, more plankton, more fish. Why birds move, chasing insects, seeds, nectar. It's a matter of twenty-three degrees, twenty-seven minutes. Tilted away from the sun in winter, toward the sun in summer. North and south, the birds move, and the whales.

Yes, I say, thinking no. I will not believe it, for then I must believe all that flows from it.

In the fall, when he headed south again, I wondered if my heart would be dislodged completely, orbiting on without me, tilted twenty-three degrees and twenty-seven minutes away from his own beating heart. While the north lay hooded with cold and dark, while the birds went field to field, following the full-ripening grain, and the whales crisscrossed the ocean's currents flush with plankton, what did Gil follow south each fall? And how long would the off-kilter tilt of his heart tip him back my way each spring?

I'll always come back, he said.

And I did believe him, against the evidence of my own heart. For the heart, like the sun, cannot alter its orbit, can burn, even when covered by cloud, even when masked by pleasure, or pain.

.

FORTY-ONE

Did I say I missed Gilly in her absence? I saved up a few things to tell her when she returns.

— Have you been pining for me? she says, barging in without knocking.

She's not a mind reader. Only a narcissist.

— You were away for what, all of six hours?

— Exactly. A really long time to go without my brilliant company. Oh go ahead, say it. You missed me.

— No. The only thing I've missed was having someone around to take the sheets off the line.

She goes out, the wind cocooning her in cotton.

— So much for clean sheets, I say when she returns, trailing them across the porch.

— Don't they smell good? she asks. I'll make up the bed later unless you want to talk to me while I'm playing housekeeper. Come on. You can help me keep Dash off the bed at least until I've finished.

— Heel, I tell Dash. Sit. Stay.

He jumps on the bed, and the two of them roll around in the pile of clean sheets. It never mattered before. Maybe I wish *she* thinks it should matter. That I should have clean sheets. That I should even sleep on sheets at all, instead of bare mattress ticking, those days when I can't be bothered to remake the bed or when I've forgotten and left them on the line in the rain.

— How am I supposed to talk over all that fuss? I say.

I join them on the bed, where she drapes a sheet around all three of us, pulling us close.

— You'll manage, she says. Go ahead, now, talk. I'm waiting.

I'll always wonder if, instead of encouraging Gil to pursue the keeper's job at the Chatham Beach Life-Saving Station, I should have left him alone. His work as a surfman there seemed to suit him. He could still carry on with his birding and fishing, his hunting and scavenging. The few months' work in storm season imposed just enough structure to smooth out his edges.

Mondays and Thursdays practice with the beach apparatus, Tuesdays boat drills, work on first aid and signaling on Wednesdays, cleaning the station on Saturdays, ordinary days contrapunted by the quickened or dying strains of wrecked ships, Sirens singing the sailors onto the outer bar. Gil must have heard their call as well, and so I imagined the allure of a chorus of enchantresses, women who, from the neck down, took on the shape of birds, mocking him seaward.

When the ocean was unruffled, he preferred solitary duty in the station's tower, watching for star trails or albatross, all the while keeping an eye out for the signal flare of any passing ship. Even calm days were no guarantee against catastrophe. One of the few deaths blotting the station's record during Gil's tenure was on a slick-calm day, when the crew was battling not wind or waves, but fire and poisonous fumes. A seaman, overcome by gas from burning lime in the hold of the schooner *Lady of the Ocean*, died in the surfboat on his way to shore. Gil, as surfman in charge in the keeper's absence, boarded the vessel and sealed the decks to keep her from bursting into flames.

Danger, then, came at ships not only from the wind tattering their sails or waves breasting their bows. At times, death came up out of the utmost bowels of the ships themselves, their cargo of lime or marble or storm-crazed cattle turned hellfire or brimstone or some bestial curse. No matter. It was all part of the life-saving crew's work, and in truth, its attraction.

This is what I tell Gilly, who is wearing the wide-wale corduroys her father favored and a white linen shirt one size too large, perhaps one I have pressed before, my spit sizzling on the flatiron as I tested its heat. So thin is the oft-washed fabric that I see her camisole, the only feminine touch about her other than her face, softened by her mother's aspect.

FORTY-TWO

WE RETURN TO THE PARLOR WHERE, part of our daily routine, Gilly accepts a cognac, as well as the opportunity to pour. In spite of all that lolling around on the unmade bed in my room, I haven't felt well today, so I lie reclined on the couch where I often sleep, the French doors behind me, the swan overhead. Gilly sits in the tufted velvet chair with its second upholstery, the interwoven hairs of the dog whose seat she has taken. The chair's red plush is now plaid with his coppery brown.

She has her own story to tell, she says, of another fire at sea, this from the first world war. The *Merlin*, a British tanker torpedoed by the Germans patrolling off Cape Hatteras in 1918, the year she was born. She tells me it's a rescue still talked about today. As she leans forward in her chair, sipping her cognac, I am pleased to say she tops up both our glasses without being bidden.

Sitting back, with long legs extended, Gilly starts to describe how the man standing watch saw the explosion—

The man standing watch, I say, the watchman on duty at Chicamacomico Station saw both the explosion and the pillar of water that rose out of a choppy sea on that overcast summer day. Chicamacomico was closer than either Oregon Inlet or Gull Shoal stations, to the north and south.

Your father was there, visiting your grandfather, Griffin O'Neal, the station's keeper. The two men had made amends, the bonds of—

— Blythe. Wake up. I think we need to start rationing your cognac.

It's not the cognac. It's the between-place I prefer more and more each day. For every black line of type in a book, there is a white space between the lines. Where the true story lies. That space holds all— the written and unwritten, the spoken and unspoken, the imagined, the unimaginable.

Shall I tell Gilly I already know the story of the *Merlin* firsthand, from one who was there, someone who showed me the burns running from his knuckles to his elbows, faint red medallions to prove he was brave, as if it were proof I needed?

Should she know that her father was a man who lived between women, faithful as the tides, north and south an ebb and flow irresistible as the pull of the moon all through its endless phases? For her father did come back, just as he said he would. That I let him is another story.

FORTY-THREE

IT WAS 1918, THE YEAR YOU WERE BORN. Your father was there, visiting your grandfather, keeper at the Chicamacomico Station. Griffin O'Neal and Gil had made amends, the bonds of the life-saving service stronger, apparently, than any domestic strife.

Gil often crossed the sound, going over to the beach to hang around the men at the station, another diversion to keep him away from Roanoke Island and the feminine turbulence of Tranquil House.

Your mother always complained how Mr. Lodge, as she called our husband, was absent for so many months after you were born that the next time he next laid eyes on his namesake, you were already able to crawl. More forgiving than I would have been, this Maud, pointing and nodding and goo-gooing at his gilt-framed portrait, diligently teaching the baby to say Papa.

Gil was still a vigorous man, as was his father-in-law, Captain O'Neal, both men close to the same age, easily belying their proximity to seventy. By then, the Life-Saving Service had become the Coast Guard and Chicamacomico had been renamed Rodanthe, but their mission, as well as the hardscrabble village, remained the same.

Calling all hands, O'Neal agreed to let Gil to join the crew, the liberty man being ill. Or perhaps the situation indeed warranted letting a man not in uniform take the lead surfman's position in the lifeboat. It was truly desperate, a tanker in flames five miles offshore.

The men ran to the stables and hitched the station's horses to the beach cart, pulling the motor lifeboat down to the surf's edge. In the effort to launch her through twenty-foot breakers, they swamped the boat three times and each time had to haul her up and bail her out. By the time she made it out to sea, it was late afternoon. It would be long after nightfall before they beached the boat with their fourth and final load of merchant seamen.

When the crew reached the ship, some seventy-five feet of water lay between her bow and stern. Not only the broken tanker, but the very sea was engulfed. Each time the surfboat crested a wave, the surfmen looked out over what could have been a forested range, its every hill and valley a shifting avalanche not of rocks but fire, the chop and heave of waves accelerating the ignition of the tanker's cargo of gasoline and diesel fuel that spread over the ocean as far as they could see.

All the British seamen had made it into the tanker's lifeboats. One boat, overloaded, capsized, spilling men into the sea. Captain Winthrop watched from a distance, and in spite of the heat, felt a terrible chill, seeing his men diving repeatedly beneath the flame-slicked water, torn between the chance to burn or boil or drown. The other sailors sat stupefied, and so the captain must have feared that unless he could somehow rouse them from their shock and disorientation, they, too, would be roasted alive. He might have shouted to them to lay on the oars, thinking he would flog their blistered backs if need be, anything to help them to save themselves. As they rowed through the flames, barrels of fuel detonated, sending geysers of burning oil skyward.

The Coast Guardsmen's surfboat picked its way through the wreckage and debris that floated and massed like burning icebergs. The crewmen had to maneuver through the black smoke, thick on the water as some rotten fog, so that at first they heard, rather than saw, the men clinging to the overturned lifeboat, feet pedaling hard to stay above the inferno, others all coated with oil, hair afire, engulfed in the viscous burning sea. Six of these they saved. The other nine, who could say, as they slipped beneath the waves, whether their lungs were filled with water or fire.

While Captain Winthrop's lifeboat waited just beyond the breakers, Griffin O'Neal began the search for the first mate's lifeboat, calculating it would likely be downwind of the *Merlin*. They found the remainder of the crew nine miles southeast of the station, and took the craft in tow.

As the surfboat headed in, Zion O'Neal shouted. There through the smoke coiling along the tops of the waves, he thought he'd seen a submarine's periscope planted like a foreign flagpole on the sea. And perhaps his eyes did touch the eyes of Kapitänleutnant Albrecht, so that two wills collided across the waves, each man sure of his own triumph, neither in doubt of the utmost worth of his cause, destruction and salvation balanced equally on the scales of human effort. Perhaps the two men offered each other a lift of the chin, one sooted with a pirate's beard, the other clean-shaven. One floating above, the other slipping beneath the orange waves.

As night fell, O'Neal's crew continued bringing men to shore, transferring them from lifeboat to surfboat, the seas too rough for the sailors to make it in on their own.

The people of Chicamacomico had become accustomed to keeping black curtains at their windows. The owner of the village's single and highly prized Model T had taped over the headlights, leaving tiny pinholes. Since June, even the beams of the Cape Hatteras and Bodie Island lighthouses had been dimmed. Anything to deprive the Germans of the least guiding light. Now gathered on the beach, indifferent or defiant, they had lit fires to lead the men home. When the first surfman came ashore with a sailor slung over his back, it was as though he had walked the survivors across a desert instead of dredging them up out of the sea. "Hot country," he said.

The boathouse looked like a burn ward, the merchant seamen swathed in gauze, shreds of their British livery carefully peeled away along with rashers of flesh. Captain Winthrop went down the rows of men, unable to put names to faces, only to count, over and over, the absence of those nine men out of the fifty-one who had sailed with him past Cape Hatteras. If one of the survivors opened his weeping and bloodshot eyes, it was as though the reflection of what he had seen continued to burn on. The eyes of the seamen and the life-savers alike were red as live coals. There in the boathouse, too, was the surf-boat, its white hull scorched, the paint blistered. The boat loomed above them like an icon or an omen.

Gold Life-Saving Medals were awarded to all the crew. Grand Crosses of Honor, the Silver Cup, King George's Victory Medal, honor heaped on honor, these men were and still are the most highly decorated of all life-savers in the history of the service.

Of course, Gil was not a recipient. This lack is part of who he ever was.

FORTY-FOUR

PERHAPS IT WAS THE DRILLS THAT FIRST DISENCHANTED HIM, in those early years when he was still just a surfman. The government encouraged keepers to make the practice rescues a community event, and all the women in Chatham seemed to think it the height of what they called "the fall season" to stroll beneath their parasols up and down the beach, white muslins trailing sand. As the crew rammed powder into the barrel of the Lyle gun or hauled the breeches buoy up the crosstrees or practiced capsizing and righting the surfboat, the women discussed each man's physique right down to his toes and commented on his prowess, judged by standards of their own making. Gil couldn't bear it.

If he couldn't be in the surfboat, hauling victims over the rail, or handing them down from a vessel's slanting and wave-sheeted deck, it was the beach patrols that suited him best. Of all the surfmen's tasks, this seemed the least like work, a welcome freedom, the solitary walk north toward Old Harbor or south toward Monomoy in pitch dark or moon-shadowed night, his mind running swift as the tide, catching the ocean's mood, soothing or turbulent by turns.

On this chopped-up bit of coast, with its one station per island, there was no exchange of check badges between surfmen. Here the idea was for a surfman to walk until he ran out of land. The first time

Gil was sent on patrol was not at night, but on a day too stormy to survey the sea from the watchtower at the station. He neither raced nor dallied, but walked steadily south toward Monomoy, keeping his eye turned east. At land's end, he walked up toward the dune to the post where a key was affixed. It must have been a relief to unfasten his oilcloth jacket, just to let in some air. It was a strange, almost tropical rain. He took the patrol clock from its leather pouch and inserted the key that would mark the paper dial to show the time, proving he had walked the full patrol.

He spent a few minutes surveying the shoal waters swirling between Nauset Beach and Monomoy, looking for signs of fish, as well as shipwrecked men. As soon as the storm subsided, the fishing would be good.

When Gil returned to the station, the keeper glanced up, laying his station log on the desk.

— Know what time it is? You think this is soft duty? Just something so's you can see if the fish are running? Captain Kendrick asked. He sat swiveling in his chair, cupped the briarwood bowl of his pipe, and let the stuck minute hand on the station clock make up lost time before continuing.

— Sure never counted you for a slacker. The letters from those Boston hunters didn't hold no sway with me, but Rafe Bishop's recommendation don't come easy, and he said you were the man for the job. I seen the way you handle a boat, ever since you were a boy, so I said why not try you out. Long as you don't bring any dead birds into this station.

Gil stood dripping, and if I know Gil, he would have continued to stand there saying nothing, just looking steadily at the man.

— Supposed to go all the way to the inlet, not on a Sunday stroll a few hundred yards down the beach. What's the matter, didn't like getting wet?

— Sir, I did go.

He took the patrol clock out and handed it to Captain Kendrick.

The keeper looked at the time stamp, and checked to see that it was Gil's clock and not someone else's.

— What'd you do, fly there?

Gil would have shrugged, and when the keeper slid his chair back, only then would he have answered.

— No sir, I walked. Spent a little time checking out the fishing grounds. Sure. Nothing running. Yet. Then came back.

He let that hang in the air, what would have been insolence, saved by the crooked half-smile, then finished.

— No ship sightings to report. Sir.

Again, the smile, half-bitten.

Kendrick looked him up and down.

— Well, you're not paid to sprint there and back. Just slow down those long legs of yours and pull a full two-hour patrol. I don't care if you have to walk there and back three times to fill up the time before you punch the clock. Get back out there and don't let me see you again until noon or I'll turn you upside down and use that stand of hair of yours to muck out Dolly's stall.

If Kenrick thought his orders were a punishment, he was wrong. Gil nodded his head, and when Kendrick swiveled his chair again, glaring over his shoulder, Gil said, Yes sir, put on his sou'wester, and went through the open double doors.

Kendrick, looking out, raised one grizzled eyebrow as Gil did a handstand, his sou'wester falling off. He crabbed sideways on his hands down the wooden boat ramp and then jackknifed onto the sand. He picked up the hat but didn't bother to put it back on. Shaking his head like a wet dog in the rain, he headed back south again. He did not shorten his stride.

Suppose, all those years ago, forty years and more, before the *Merlin* and so many other wrecks, north and south, had taken their toll, the prevailing winds had been laying down along their accustomed track, veering out of the northeast as Gil made his way up Nauset Beach. He would have been walking, head down, bent over at the waist to gain traction, the wind's force contorting his body. He reveled in it. He was invincible. His oilskins collected a glistening second skin of ice. His sou'wester useless, he held a shingle in front of his face to ward off the stinging sand and sleet intermingled, his frozen mittens shaped into tight fists that cracked across the knuckles whenever he flexed his fingers to get the blood flowing or when he flattened one palm to turn a cartwheel on the beach, in defiance or delight or both, that strange and unsettling mixture of opposing moods that, for me, was the solution to the equation, the sum total of his attraction.

The drills, the watches, the patrols—these things, combined with the intensity of storm when all came together for good or ill, wrecked or saved, seemed to me a good balance between noble effort and unfocused indulgence. But Gil ever had his own ideas.

FORTY-FIVE

WHY I THOUGHT GIL COULD TAKE ORDERS from Washington any better than he could from the keeper in charge at Chatham Beach Station, I can't say. Gil got along fine with the crew but he had trouble bending to the will of others. Especially when he thought he was right, and when was it otherwise? Nevertheless, it was my mistake.

When the keeper's post came available, I encouraged him to apply. He was well recommended by all my father's colleagues, as well as his own following of influential Boston men. Theodore Sparrow, the district superintendent, was concerned about his youth, but he had comported himself so well as a surfman, moving from eighth to first rank in five years, that he received the appointment.

Gil wasted no time. As soon as he was appointed keeper, he wrote to Washington seeking approval for an invention he called a faking box, a wooden crate containing a frame with long wooden pegs arranged on the periphery. His hope, no, his assumption, was that it would be approved for use not only at Cape Cod's own district of twelve stations but also at stations throughout the entire life-saving service.

When seas were too rough for the surfboat, the first line of communication between the life-savers and a wrecked ship was literally a line, or a rope, attached to a projectile that was shot from a small cannon out to the ship. The shot line would then be rigged with a whip line and block, which acted like a clothesline on pulleys running between the beach and the ship. The whip line could haul a tally board with instructions to the ship's crew, or a breeches buoy to transport crew and passengers just above the cresting waves, or if the wreck were close in, the beach cart could be ferried out to the ship.

All the townspeople were familiar with this operation, for it was part of an autumn day's drill. Until now, Gil had been reticent about the box. It would either work or it wouldn't. For Gil it was enough, the knowing where and how to pull a bird down out of the sky or a fish up from the deeps, it was enough to feel the rhythm of a rescue, knowing how to time a wave, rushing the sea with all oars lifted, muscle and wood and wave stepping in time with the precision of a minuet. Acclaim or even the slightest notice made the music stop for Gil, leaving him standing in the middle of the floor, red-faced. But now he worked on his invention not caring who knew. That he might need approval to save lives would never have occurred to him.

His idea, then, was to fake or coil the shot line in a diagonal pattern around the pegs. The line, when carefully pushed off the pegs, would reel out without tangling as it flew above the breaking seas and across the ship's bow. As it presently stood, if the line fouled, the rope would have to be hauled back through rank upon rank of twenty-foot breakers, up and out of the cloying surf, rewound back into a coil, retied to the projectile, and then shot out again.

He had heard how some eighty-five men aboard the *Metropolis* had drowned down south, near the Currituck Beach Life-Saving Station in Carolina. The keeper had brought only two charges of powder in his flask and failed to get the first line out, and then, pure bad luck, the second shot-line parted.

Even with plenty of black powder and a dead-on aim, Gil himself had seen ships break apart and men drop one by one from mast or crossbeams down into the sea while the life-saving crew repeatedly shot the line, only to see it stop short, jerked into a snarled, wet heap. His design, he thought, would send the line flying in one smooth un-raveling. He said he'd be damned before he'd see a crew ridiculed by some congressman claiming the Newfoundland dog that had swum out and dragged a half-drowned man ashore from the wreck of the *Metropolis* was braver than the Currituck Beach crew who, in the end, had pulled more than a hundred and fifty living souls from the surf. Then after you've waded through all the red tape they can throw at you, he said, here come the letters from the dead men's families, asking what were their last words:

FORTY-SIX

THE FAKING BOX HAD TAKEN SEVERAL MONTHS TO PERFECT. The box wasn't big enough, the line too long, the pegs too tall or too short. Ben's voice nagged him: Use your head before you use your hands and you'll save time and materials. Think of it as extra time to fish.

Gil sketched out a design on the back of a government envelope, thinking, See, Ben, I even saved paper.

He'd worked on it all summer, and now he was in no mood for an audience, or at least an official one. On a day when the keeper was away, he hitched Dolly to the cart loaded with the usual beach apparatus—Lyle gun, rope, powder, shot—and his precious box. He was finally ready to test his contraption that looked, to me, like some cat's cradle. The seventeen wooden spindles held an immense length of rope, six hundred yards' worth, equal to a dozen schooners set end to end.

The braided linen line, so soft when loosely held, could burn a bloody crease in your palm when it whipped behind the cast-iron projectile, the kick of the small cannon so violent that just an ounce or two of powder would knock the gun back six feet.

The drill mast, complete with crow's nest, was set up some five hundred yards down the beach from the station, something to aim for, stand-in for a ship's mainmast. The faking box was more than one person could handle, so I had to help Gil turn the box upside down and lift off the frame containing the wooden pins. The rope with its neatly coiled loops or fakes remained in the box, ready to unspool. We tipped the box at a forty-five-degree angle toward the imaginary ship that in my mind was filled with a dozen or more desperate men, and perhaps there was a captain's wife lashed to the mast ten feet above the submerged deck, clutching a figmentary child, its feeble screams swallowed by the wind.

Gil unhitched Dolly and used her to pull the Lyle gun down out of the cart and into position, a few feet to windward of the faking box. When it was time to light the fuse, I went to watch from the station's tower. I climbed the ladder and stood looking down, adjusting my spyglass until the sweat gathering at his temples came into focus. The expression on his face would tell far more of the success of his experiment than any rope could.

There on the empty beach, Gil charged the Lyle gun with eight ounces of Hazard's black powder, the full charge for a rescue, not just the ounce and a half used in training drills. In spite of all the talk of the *Metropolis* and men lost for lack of powder, he'd filled his flask with just a single charge. He threaded the end of the thin rope line through the eye of the shot and loaded the projectile into the gun's short barrel. All this was routine, practiced hundreds of times over the past five years.

The gun's reverberation caused me to jerk the spyglass. I saw the rope uncoil like a string singing its kite skyward. When I finally focused on Gil, there he went, turning handstands down the beach. He tumbled across the sand and right into the sea, triumphant and sleek.

FORTY-SEVEN

When the keeper's job came open, then, perhaps it was the chance to put his invention to use and not so much my own urging that caused him to apply for the post. At least that's what I told myself later, when all went wrong and I regretted ever wanting to see him wear the keeper's insignia.

His men loved the contraption. The first time he used it, they looked at him like he was a snake charmer drawing a cobra up out of its straw basket. Now that his aim was no longer hostage to the rope's unwinding, it seemed he never missed, neither in drills nor rescues, and each time, one of the surfmen would carve a notch in the box, until it was crosshatched with cuts.

It had been months since he'd written to Washington. As he waited for an answer, I had to listen to his complaints, how the service was becoming just another pencil-pushing, rule-spawning, ingenuity-stifling excuse for a paycheck. Since the wreck of the *Metropolis*, he was worse. He wouldn't stop ranting about Sargent, a senator from California, late of our own Newburyport, who tried his best to transfer the Service from Treasury to the Navy.

— Like we need proper "military discipline." It's gotten bad enough already, telling us what time to eat and how to dress, right down to our toes. Trousers rolled up or stuffed into boots other than hip boots, "positively forbidden." Let them come out on these blazing hot sands and march up and down, setting up for a drill. Let a wave smack them and see how they like clammy wet cloth sticking to their legs while trying to beat the last man's time climbing the drill mast. I could care less whether the men roll up their trousers. They can go naked for all I care, so long as they jump to it when I call.

For Gil, that was quite a speech. I asked him if he carried on this way at the station, afraid somehow it would get back to headquarters.

— No. Only you. Only to you, he said, brushing the backs of two fingers against my cheek, before walking out the door.

Just a few words, a few seconds of looking directly into my eyes, the barest touch. It sustained me.

FORTY-EIGHT

IT'S RAINING, SO GILLY AND I HAVE BEEN INDOORS, looking at news clippings about various rescues. There's an article from the local paper about the history of the Life-Saving Service.

— Here, look at this, she says. They're talking about the Blue Book, the official rules.

— "The Blue Book says you have to go out. It doesn't say anything about coming back," I quote from memory.

— Exactly. Well, not exactly, Gilly says. It was Cap'n Pat Etheridge who said it. And he used the word "damn." As in, "It doesn't say a damn thing about coming back." He made that comment when a surfman was kicking up a fuss about going out to a wreck off Diamond Shoals. Cap'n Pat's my uncle, he was keeper at the Cape Hatteras station. I didn't know that saying had made it all the way up here.

— I remember Gil coming back from one of his trips south, quoting that line. Just one more connection Gil made between these capes, I say. He should have been in the import/export business.

— Maybe that's how that saying made it into the Blue Book.

— No. He didn't think you even needed a rule book.

— Let's sit on the porch and watch the rain, Gilly says. I'm ready to hear more stories.

— All right.

The weather suits my mood, reminds me of a day when the weather was sunny but Gil's mood was not.

It was one of those afternoons, a day so bright, the sun cast everything in exact duplicate, making you want to reach out and shake hands with your shadow. I'd come to the station with Dash, hoping to entice Gil to go for a walk. He was sitting on a crate, chin in his hands. He'd just opened a letter from headquarters.

— Bad news? They didn't approve the use of your faking box at all the other stations?

He stood and shoved the crate across the floor with his foot.

— What's in the box? I asked.

— The Blue Book says you have to go out, never mind coming back. And now, apparently, the Blue Book says I'm to become a monkey shimmying up a pole. I'm starting not to give a damn about any of it.

I don't say a word, make my face a blank, eyes soft, so he can say out loud what he feels. It's better if he can. That often he can't is proved by the inward slant of his brows, the line between them a permanent feature except when he's on the water or when he lets me smooth it free with my fingers.

— No doubt about it. Being a surfman was better. Do what you're told, go out when a ship sends up a flare, do a few practice drills even if it has to be in front of those awful women. But then the rest of the day is yours.

Gil took a claw hammer from his toolbox and pried the lid from a crate stenciled with his name and his post.

— Now it's reading letters, writing letters, yes, your shipment of moldy potatoes received, no we didn't eat them, not with good Cape reds hilled over in the fields.

He stood looking down into the crate sent from headquarters. Inside was sloppily coiled wire that would carry words clicking along

its length. He picked up the instructions that lay atop the wire, speci-
fying the kind, height, and diameter of poles and cross arms, how
many feet apart, how deep to dig the holes in the sand. A transmitter
and codebook lay in the tangled wire, with yet another set of instructions. The letter contained a deadline for installation, and the test
message Gil was instructed to transmit when the job was complete,
a quote from the first telegram sent by Samuel Morse himself: *What
hath God wrought?*

FORTY-NINE

For an entire week, Gil did the unthinkable for a lifesaver. Working parallel to the shore, he kept his back to the sea. At least then he wouldn't be confronted by the blot on the horizon. Poles and wire now stretched north from Chatham Beach Station to Orleans and south to Monomoy.

So it would be that his men would keep well clear of him and take care not to show their interest in the telegraph key or codebook. Whenever he walked into the day room or onto the porch they would stop their incessant practice, tapping index finger to wrist or spoon to plate. If they were too late and he caught them at it, they would begin whistling, as though he'd only walked in on a boisterous rendition of "Cheerily Man."

These men who would follow him without hesitation into the surf, to save lives, yes, but more, to live up to his expectation of them, they were skilled at keeping a weather eye and could see one of Gil's thunderheads building.

It might have been Mackey who said, Come on, Cap'n, join us, as he tossed a harmonica across the room. Gil's arm would have stretched out to catch it, hand moving smoothly to mouth. Say that knuckles, spoons, shoe leather caught the rhythm of "Farewell and

Adieu." I imagine Gil's lips moving along the ridged chambers to the music of inhale and exhale, just as I've felt them move down my spine.

The fo'c's'le shanty's refrain came to an end. Cahoon spoke up.

— Heard the *Lilac* sailed nineteen days ago, should be making Pollock Rip tomorrow.

Heads turned toward Gil, and then all eyes looked down. The men had tapped the test message a dozen times, sly as old women repeating the same gossip from fence post to porch step. At last, real news had come in fits and starts along the wire. They waited for Gil to cloud up, but if he thought about how they already knew of the *Lilac*'s departure six ports south of Chatham, he didn't show it.

Gil tossed the harmonica back to Mackey, then answered Cahoon.

— Pity, then. A front's coming. No man would want the weather that's building. This one's running in at us on a Proxigean tide.

He cuffed Barney's ear.

— To you, that means the spring tide's going to be high, really high, you good-for-nothing excuse for a sailor. The blues are going to be running ahead of the storm. Let's hope the *Lilac*'s heavy laden, slow her down, give her a few days' leeway.

— And you a few days' fishing, said Mackey.

— You're your own weathervane, now that's the God's honest truth, Barney said, grabbing Gil's wrist and twisting it behind his back before spinning him about, Gil feigning a reeling stumble across the room, arms outstretched, the men laughing.

That night the moon, all socketed tight in a metallic haze, confirmed Gil's forecast. An hour later, the clouds had sopped up the last of the moon's light so that even the whitecaps lacked their proper shine atop the bulking waves that could not be seen, their ionic power only felt, deep in the blood's salt echo.

Gil told Mackey he would take the watch.

— That's all right, I don't mind, Mackey said. My pap would always tell me, "Long foretold, long last. Short notice, soon past." You've been saying for days weather was building. Going to be a long night, and we'll not see the last of it for a while.

None of the men would sleep, the glass falling, the barometric pressure affecting them like strong coffee.

As all the men knew he would, Gil finally turned to Cahoon.

— So did that contraption tell you how many passengers and crew?

Cahoon was the oldest of the surfmen, a dozen years older than Gil. He hitched his sleeves, shucked his collar, and then stroked his gray beard, tapering to white, which reached four buttons down his chest.

— Well, Cap, it's like this, he said. We ain't yet learned the Morse code for numbers.

This would be when Gil smiled, teeth gleaming in a five-day growth of beard. He would push up off the floor, where he was sitting cross-legged, and say, Go on, get some rest. I'll be counting on all of you tomorrow.

Off he would go, down the beach, a black slash against a blacker night, consumed in a rising wind.

FIFTY

Dawn arrived in tatters, the beach strewn with what Gil thought was seaweed. As a weakling sun lifted out of waves notched high on the horizon, he saw it was not Sargasso weed or kelp, no wrack line but the torn bodies of birds. He picked up a one-winged bird, another, its neck thinly garroted, and another, its breast feathers slashed. Not storm wrack. The tide had not reached this high. The line of mutilated birds ran down the beach nearly as far as he could see.

— What in hell's name, he said. The birds seemed to answer, a gust of wind lifting a wing here and there, pointing up toward the black wire running parallel to the shore like a guillotine poised for another bloody descent.

A dopping of red phalaropes, dozens of them, had made a rare appearance over land. The birds mostly lived at sea, unless racing ahead of a storm or coming ashore to lay their blotched olive eggs. Gil wasn't surprised by their arrival—in fact, he expected them, yet another sign of weather building out of the southeast. But the sight of the birds' lovely throats edged with pale ochre, now a gashy red, made him sick.

Suppose a gust of wind caught a bird and resurrected it, spinning it around. Perhaps it would have reminded him of how we'd once seen phalaropes fishing for their supper at Oyster Pond on one of their short stays ashore.

We had watched the birds swim in a tight, pot-stirring circle, pulling food up into the vortex, dinner served. Laughing, he'd fallen back on the bank, grabbed a stick, and spun it in the water. See, Blythe, he said, the birds just have to go around and around, one easy step, caught, cooked, and eaten, even you could do it. See why a flock's sometimes called a twirl or a whirligig? I've heard old-timers tell how they've seen fish sucked right out of the ocean and up into the sky on a waterspout. Same thing. Now, as to why they say, Here comes a dopping of reds, I don't know, guess it's like a wisp of snipes. One of your collective nouns, isn't it, Madame Grammarian?

He could go on forever about anything that had the least relation to a sky filled with mackerel scales or mares' tails, or hold forth on the subject of any rogue wave fetched up out of a rip current or a slacking tide. And once, there'd been a time when he could never get his fill of this face, these brows delicate as moth fringe, he said, and the even flare of teeth whose sharpness he would test with his tongue, and these secretly dimpled limbs, however he would arrange them, smoothing every crease. He was forever enamored of the habits of currents and skies. My habits, as well, I'd thought. Who is to say what lasts.

Shall I say, then, how Gil would have walked the beach, over-turning birds with the tip of his boot? He would have picked up a phalarope, one of the few without a torn wing, and examined it. His fingers would play over the bird's short legs and lobed feet, its strong, flat bill greenish yellow, like Ben's Chartreuse. He would stroke the white stripe running along its cheek and then turn the bird over, smoothing the feathers that helped name it, a red softly veined as the inside of a rabbit's ear.

What would the birds look like to the whales that swam below them far out to sea, surfacing to have their mossy hides scratched by the eager beaks of the phalaropes, they in turn glad to alight on the whales' humped backs, big as any farmer's field?

He looped a turn of his belt around the bird's feet and walked farther, looking for a specimen he could mount. This one he would float in seawater, in a glass container, so that he could see what the whales saw, whether the bird's bronzy red breast, refracted through crystals of salt, would flash bright crimson.

He stopped, still astonished by the slaughter wreaked by one thin wire. He thought of discarding this bird among the rest, sand crabs' fodder. Why float it in glass, hold it up to the light? He could never know whether his own seeing was the same as the whales', whether their eyes translated light into the same language. Perhaps they saw green where he saw red, or some other spectrum his own eye could not unprism.

Shedding his oilskins, he unfastened the bird from his belt. A wave came to meet him, a quick chop at the back of his knees then a punch to his stomach, and it was as though the phalarope were in league with the sea, wanting them both to go down under to that tempestuous place where pearls could become eyes all seeing. The ocean was as cold as the bird's unbeating heart. The shock of it startled Gil alive. He waded out, the bird held overhead in two hands, facing the wind. As the next comber rushed the shore, he and the bird dived smoothly into the foamed vortex, spinning through the turbulence, he with eyes wide open, seeing whale.

When next he walked on land, no bird at his belt, he came to one of the poles already leaning like a drunkard boozy with wind. He shimmied barefoot to the top. Pulling his knife from its sheath, he cut the telegraph wire, a frisson of electricity running up his arm and tingling deep into the roots of his jaw teeth. The line fell down onto the wreckage of birds, the wind lifting their feathers as though reincarnated in one last remembrance of flight.

What hath *man* wrought? he thought. That should have been the first message you ever sent, Samuel Morse, never mind God.

He thought of the men, their tapping fingers, signaling nothing. What did it matter, after all, whether they knew the *Lilac* had sailed, and on what day, or with what cargo. She, and others, would make their way or not. The Outer Bar and Pollock Rip would be waiting, and so would he and his men.

FIFTY-ONE

I HAVE BEEN THERE AT CHATHAM BEACH BEFORE, have aided passengers or crew after they've been dragged ashore, then carried by two men, arms crossed and hands clasped to make a sling, juddering the poor souls a mile or more up the beach to the station.

A young woman might be sitting there by the stove, its door open, throwing heat. She would tremble from cold, but even more from fright. My fingers sting as I take hold of auburn ringlets rimed white that clack and glisten with each jolt of her body. I break the frozen curls apart like icicles hanging rigid from an eave. Her teeth chattering, she recalls the waves. Mountains of water that ranged alongside the schooner, sea cliffs so tall, she says, they would have put the ship in shadow had there been a sun.

Mountains, even in earthquakes or avalanches, do not gather themselves and grow taller. They do not rush up out of yesterday's flat terrain. Seas are not mountains. They can move from flat calm to towering crest, leaving splintered ships in their wake.

Still, men can be counted on to believe they're invincible. Ships will sail, even though the sea bulges and sucks, gnashes and swallows, spawning monstrous new waves out of the constancy of the deep.

I speak of this to Gil.

He listens, shrugs. Waves are just water, he says. Isn't that enough?

FIFTY-TWO

— WHAT? GILLY ASKS. What was that about mountains?

— I don't know what you're talking about.

— Mountains. You said something about mountains falling down. And a woman with icicles instead of hair. Were you dreaming or something, Blythe?

— If you don't know, how am I supposed to? You're supposed to be listening. You're the one who's fallen asleep, not me.

— I. Don't. Think. So.

— Don't be impertinent. Do you want to hear more or don't you? I can always go get some paint.

— Paint? For what?

— Well, this house could use a coat.

She lets out a most unladylike bellow.

— This house would fall down if you put a coat of paint on it, she says. I have a feeling you're a much better storyteller than house painter. Go ahead.

I get up and leave. I don't go far. Just far enough to fetch something from the windowsill. I come back with a bird wing that's seen better days.

— Here. I'll tell you about the day Gil put this wing over the door.

She picks it up with two fingers. Dash jumps up and takes it out of her hand. It falls to pieces in his mouth. Between those two, nothing is safe.

FIFTY-THREE

GIL HAD COME HOME LONG ENOUGH to tack a bird's wing, somewhat be-draggled, except for the blaze of a jagged white stripe, over the door. Long enough to tell me how saltwater had turned the bronze to crimson, lighting it up like a signal flare, so the whales could surely see. See what, I asked, but he threw a few things into his sea bag and went out the door.

I followed him. I wanted to watch Gil work this storm. I put on the oilskins he'd worn as a boy, stuffed biscuits and a flask in one pocket, my spyglass in another, and tucked a piece of tarred canvas under my arm.

The wind had blown the water out of the harbor, allowing me to walk directly to the station across what was once bottom, the silt studded with clamshells and lead sinkers, two left boots, a briarwood pipe, an occasional tree stump to mark where dry land and not shoal water once lived. It was like pulling back the covers to find a stray sock or barrette, signs of past turbulence now revealed, the secret life of sea or bed, lying beneath the sheeted currents.

I could see Gil just beyond the upwash, one of a row of men miniature against the towering breakers. He stood with his chin thrust into the neck strap of his oilcloth coat. He and his six surfmen faced south, arrayed like a V of geese to forge a break in the wind. He would never think to look up toward the dune. Besides, as I lay flat in the lee of the dune with the sailcloth wrapped around me to keep off the rain, I was invisible. Heaped over with sand that plumped me out on my windward side, I was as wide-bodied as Dolly, who stood head down by the cart, her mane streaming, her tail whipped around her leg like unbraided rope. When I leveraged my arm to reach into my pocket for the flask and a biscuit, the sand shifted and then re-molded to my shape.

The scene below me was far different from a fair-weather drill, women on promenade, children turning somersaults or slinging handfuls of sand. It always amused me to watch the men from town shifting in idle groups, how they would turn their eyes but not their heads to watch the surfmen, as though a direct gaze were some form of compliment. Now there were no celebratory crowds, only me, spy-ing out from under the flap of canvas.

I felt secure as an oyster lying long in my hinged abode, accreted with tidal lappings of gray shell laid down by waves overreaching themselves, my whole being outstretched, no pearl gathering itself around a gritted speck, no irritant beauty yet unborn. My body vi-brated, and perhaps vibration is the way an oyster hears, the jellied muscle itself all ears. Perhaps it hears a sound of its own making, like the song of a conch, or the song of a babe floating placid in the yet unbroken waters of the womb.

I listened to wind and surf outshouting each other until the sound was neither water nor air, a soporific clamor that lulled me. The men's slow and deliberate movements, the ship's torn sails streaming in long pennons, mesmerized, or it might have been the half-empty flask that made my eyes feel heavy.

To bring myself back to the scene at hand, I flipped back the canvas. I may as well have dived headlong into the sea. I was wet in an instant, rain, spray, and blowing sand stinging my face.

The crew had unloaded the cart, each apparatus familiar in its shape, but now, ranged there on the shore, the Lyle gun seemed threatening, the crotch pole and sand anchor, the hawsers and heaving stick like instruments of torture, not rescue. The breeches buoy sat at the ready, but with its life ring sagged down around the canvas pants bereft of any survivor.

I could see the ocean was too rough for the surfboat. The faking box would certainly be put to the test. The crew routinely loaded it onto the cart now, even though Gil had never received government approval. They would have to shoot a line across the ship's bow. A member of the shipwrecked crew would tie the line to a stanchion or mast. Then the lifesavers would haul in the men, one by one, dangling above the waves in the canvas breeches.

The wind was so strong Gil had to use his body like a sail or rudder just to move. He began to pace, if it could be called that, staggering back and forth like a man weighted down with an anvil, attempting to walk in deep sand. I soon saw his dilemma. The surf was running so high up the beach that he had no way to bury the sand anchor. Without the anchor, there was no way to secure the shoreside line. They would not be able to use the breeches buoy.

I saw Cahoon and Mackey flailing their arms. Gil was not one you flailed at. When he started taking off his oilskins and threw his sou'wester into the cart, I wanted to rise up out of my tent and flail my arms as well. I realized what the crew already knew. He was going to swim out to the ship. The men backed away as if he were a dead man upright.

For once Gil was not graceful. He struggled to keep his footing in the surf. There was no way he could see, rain and spume hitting him full in the face like buckets of water being slung down a fire line. Waves were running in on a sloppy crosscurrent chop, the longshore and nearshore currents colliding with great cymbals of spray.

He continued to struggle up and down the beach, and I first thought he was trying to time his run into the combers, whose crests were blown backward even as the waves hollowed themselves into caverns of water that collapsed from their own weight and forward momentum. But he was looking for something.

He and I saw it at the same time—the telltale band of color, the spume trail running out to sea, the cross-chopped waves like two palms clapping. I realized what he was about to attempt. I didn't know whether to stand up and cheer or bury my head under the canvas. Gil intended to ride a rip current out to the ship.

FIFTY-FOUR

EVEN THOUGH IT WAS MIDDAY, a lowering sky struggled to reflect the sea, tinged with storm. Both sea and sky were like an artist's palette dabbed with paints, thin smears of lamp black and Payne's gray, with only the smallest hint of cobalt. I could barely see the vessel, perhaps a sloop. She was aground on the bar, you could tell by the rake of her prow, white water breaking all around her. A sudden ray of sun glinted bright against the bruised and aching clouds.

I could see the undercurrent rushing seaward between a break in the sandbar. My mind ran with the echo of Ben's words, Gil going on about the Bernoulli effect, the rip current swift as a China clipper, all sails set.

Gil saw, or more likely felt the riptide, and moved into it. In an instant, he was gone.

I was too anxious to stay buried in my bed of sand, peering out from under the canvas. As if standing up would put me closer to Gil, I stood with my elbow braced at my waist, steadying the glass in my palm. In the ocean's disarray there was no way I could find him, but then he emerged far beyond the breakers in thigh-deep surf, half walking, half swimming in the ebb and flow crossing the bar. When a wave would break, he would dive under it, coming up with the familiar shake of his head, slinging water.

Now I could see she was a sloop, with a single mast, so not the *Lilac*, a three-masted schooner. Was there even anyone on board? I saw Gil stand up and wave before he was knocked down and tumbled a few yards. Part of the splintered mast seemed to peel away. It was a man making his way to starboard. He carried something a little smaller than a seaman's duffle.

Gil pantomimed, arms outstretched, then forming a cradle. The man dropped the bundle over the side. Gil leaned in to catch it, and then moved into the lee of the ship, away from the rip current. You could see him step off the bar: one minute he was forging through shoal water and the next he'd dropped like an anchor. He surfaced, tucked the bundle under one arm, and began sidestroking toward shore.

He rode the current out four more times, bringing in first a woman, then the mate, a seaman, and finally the captain. The life-saving crew stood in a line like a bucket brigade, passing them along. Barney carried the woman to the beach cart. Her arms gestured weakly, reaching for her child or else to tear at her hair, which hung in wet matted shrouds. The captain could stand on his own, but moved as though he were a pugilist, staggering about, jabbing air, his arms unable to straighten, wrapped for so long around the mast, clutching wife and child. When they reached the cart and she was handed the boy, she ran her hands all over him as if to make sure he was whole, or that he was hers. But then she turned, shrieking toward the sea.

It would not be until later that the captain's wife finally made them understand there was another child, a baby, who'd been swept from her arms.

Yes, her babe was lost, but at least she'd once held him, had rocked him, had sung him to sleep. How do you envy that which you believe is already yours, if not by virtue of conception then of deliverance? Gil and I alone would come to know that child's fate, yet another secret that bound us even as it came between us, as only sorrow can.

FIFTY-FIVE

WHILE THE CREW WAS PREOCCUPIED with the wreck victims, it seemed everyone had forgotten Gil. Frantic, I scanned the sea, but it was difficult to see anything, even through my glass. Fog was setting in, as though the seafoam were not content with being ocean and now longed to become air. Through the intermingled foam and fog I saw long legs tumbling like pants in a washtub, arms languid as empty sleeves, a blank face sudsy with brine. At that moment, Mackey saw him and went running, the other men close behind. Thank God, I thought. That fellow's brought more than one dead man back to life.

Before Mackey could reach him, my clever, clever boy bounded up, slinging water, reeling and laughing. I felt anguish overwashed by relief, then exasperation, swept away by joy. His men clapped him on the back. Their halloos reached me far up the beach. Who could resist the mighty Cap'n Lodge, solemn jokester, reckless and brave.

I slipped over the dune and headed for the station, which stood square and red, its watchtower trailing wisps of fog. The fire was nearly out, so I stoked the woodstove with two splits of cedar, the resin and salt mingling blue flame in amongst the embers stirred back to life. The cook's rank piece of salt codfish skin tossed into the coffee pot had done nothing to clear the morning's stale and oily brew. I put more grounds on to boil, breaking an egg into the blue enamelware pot to enrich the coffee, then crushed the eggshell and dropped it in to clear the sediment.

I went upstairs, past the crew's room, their cots neat, and entered the room reserved for rescued passengers and crew. Gil had put it to double duty, also using it as the station's library. Donated by the American Seaman's Friend Society, the same books had been there for years. Gil had supplemented them with his own books, but he and Mackey were the only ones who read them. Even so, they were well-used.

The stack of clothing from the Women's Relief Society contained a good selection of sizes. I chose a few things and laid them out in the dayroom. Gil, too, would need dry clothes. I went back downstairs to the keeper's quarters and shook out a rumpled shirt stuffed under his pillow, no doubt a prop for reading in bed, and then fished out a pair of pants lying in a pile of both clean and dirty clothes shoved in a corner. For someone so worried about a rope's untidy coil or a shell out of place in his gun box or beggar's lice clinging to Dash's legs, he was always careless of himself.

Downstairs, the fire was burning, a simple domestic scene, and yet somehow disturbing, belying all I had witnessed, life and death riding tandem on a single wave. I held my hands to the fire, turned like a planet in orbit of its sun, the two halves of my body islands on opposite sides of the globe, one a floating berg, the other lathered in a tropic jungle swelter. My thoughts, too, at odds with one another. I longed for a temperate state of mind.

FIFTY-SIX

Before Gil and the crew returned with their wards, I slipped out and went to the rear of the station. Why, I couldn't say, for now was when I would usually be helping the victims, comforting them with coffee and warm clothes and simple companionship. I saw Gil step onto the porch, bending over to pick up the sheet of canvas I had dropped. He folded it once, then again, and went inside. The men brought Captain Best, his crew, and his wife and son into the dayroom.

I watched the familiar scene through the fogged window. Did they wonder why the coffee was hot or who had selected a lady's dress, petticoats, and shawl, a man's shirt, coat, and trousers, a little boy's wool dress with tiny buttons running down the front, with matching pantalets?

Dash headed straight for his bowl and began eating the food I'd put out. He ate as though he'd swum out to the ship with Gil all four times. If Barney hadn't held him back, he would have plunged in, his thick tail a rudder, his chest cleaving waves until his heart burst. Now that Gil was safe, Dash played in his water bowl. He lifted his coppery head and looked up at the window where I was standing, but he didn't give me away, content to turn back to his bowl and blow bubbles as if he were diving for oysters in the bay.

From outside, the dayroom looked cheerful, the men relieved, the survivors slowly recovering from the shock of their ordeal. I saw Gil cross the room to speak to the woman, who paced in a circle clutching her child, the wet floor mapping her anguish. She looked at Gil and made her assessment. She handed the boy to him, watched for a few more moments as he sat in his chair, dandling the toddler on his knee. She and her husband went with Barney, who walked up the steps behind them, ready to catch them if they fell. Holding to one another, they carefully placed one foot and then the other on each step, before moving to the next.

While the captain and his wife were upstairs changing into dry clothes, Gil started the child laughing, tickling him under his chin, making faces, all the silly horseplay I had imagined him using to entertain our twins.

One, two,
Three, four, five,
Once I caught a fish alive,
Six, seven,
Eight, nine, ten,
Then I let it go again.
Why did you let it go?
Because it bit my finger so.
Which finger did it bite?
This little finger on the right.

I could read Gil's lips moving in time to the rhythmic lift of his knee. I could see him bite the boy's finger, could see the boy throw his head back, laughing.

Gil deftly stripped off the child's wet clothes, stood him on the table, and put on the soft woolens I had just held to my breast, had just crushed to my face, breathing into the knitted and purled neck, nuzzling only air.

FIFTY-SEVEN

I AM BARREN. I remember the day when this thought seared my brain.

We lost the twins five months after our marriage, two tiny beings easily held, one in each hand. When one year, and another, and another went by, I kept the thought away and Gil never spoke of it.

Such a strange word, barren. It makes me think of unplowed fields, dirt bereft of rain, of an empty landscape, not a person or a tree or a wave to break the monotony, a flat beach, flaccid sea, forlorn yellow sky draining my world hopeless. And yet when I apply the word to myself, even as I think of what others have said about me for years, barren then becomes not some sere or vapid expanse but a bloody core, a hard fist that squeezes the lifeblood from me each time the moon rises up out of the ocean to peer in the window at our fruitless lovemaking, mocking my belly so flat.

In my mind I am not barren. I see Gil, arms swinging loosely from his shoulders, each strong, narrow hand holding a small fist— Gil and two other people wholly of our making, coming up the beach, eager to enfold me. We stand and embrace, sixteen chambers of a single heart, beating love.

FIFTY-EIGHT

As USUAL IN THE AFTERMATH OF A RESCUE, *Gil would be sleeping at the station that night. I made my way down the beach to his* shanty. I would sleep there, with his birds all in a row, until the storm tide receded.

Now that night was falling against an already black horizon, anything pale shone out stark as white chalk overlaid on a charcoal sketch.

I saw something rolling in the wash. It was a bolt of cloth. I dragged it and two others high on the beach, sturdy unbleached muslin that Gil would like. From it I could make brand-new shirts soft as if I had washed them a thousand times. The sea makes a good laundress.

Another smaller bolt lay above the tideline, its edge flapping feebly in the wind. But there was nothing feeble about this wind, which was still screaming in the shrouds of the abandoned sloop half a mile away.

As I approached, the roll of cloth kicked. That is, my eyes finally saw not what they expected, sodden muslin, but what I never could have imagined: an infant the sea had swaddled tight in its linen gown. What I had thought was the bolt end flapping must have been the babe's foot, but surely it was only the sea playing with its prey, strangling it in tendrils of foam, and not a live child kicking back the cold, its limbs jolting reflexively.

I scooped up the baby, who had been tied to a bit of planking. Only after I pressed it to my breast, enveloping it between oilskins and the merino wool of my fisherman's sweater, could I tell it was crying, that kind of soundless cry that works the chest like a tiny bellows heaving air. I ran to the shanty, which I knew would be well-stocked with wood, and built a fire. The small space warmed quickly once the cedar kindling caught. I sat cross-legged on the floor, the baby on a down pillow in my lap.

In the brassy play of the flames, the baby at first seemed fine, but when I took the wet gown off, the child's skin was blue, the same purplish-blue as blood running in a delta of veins at the wrist. The juddering cries were becoming sporadic, like a wobbly spinning top winding down. I tried chafing its skin to no avail, and finally thrust it against my own skin inside my sweater, and sat rocking back and forth, humming deep in my throat, a conch's lullaby thrum that turned to a shriek when Gil pulled him from me.

This babe was bigger than my two, born too soon into this world. Those boys I call Harding and Winstead, named for each of us. I do not see them, their small blue fists, do not distinguish, are they clutching at life or are they pummeling death. They run and skip in the surf, our toes seek out clams breathing softly in their shells. They help me deadhead the roses. I never hear them, except when they cry, and that is when I must go to the cliff where the ocean drowns all sound. Now there are three voices to hush.

FIFTY-NINE

GIL USED TO SAY HE WOULD BRING ME A GIFT, *something precious, a surprise.* If I got better, he said. Better than what, I would ask. He would stroke my hair. If it were up, his fingers would find the pins and release them. If it were already loose on my shoulders, he would gather blond strands and wrap them around his fist and pull, tilting my head. He would look into my eyes then as if searching for something hidden, in the marbled irises, or deeper. Then kiss my forehead and murmur You'll be better. And I would murmur back, I am better than best. I have you. This would always surely please him—a moistness would appear at the corners of his eyes, telling me without words, *Yes.*

It was usually before or after the promise of a gift that I might find him sitting with his cedar box in which he kept a tintype of Ben, along with a toy boat his brother had carved, and a few torn bits of telegram, minus the black star. That there might have been other pictures, other trinkets, how was I to know?

And what more gifts did I need? I had the jagged white blaze of a bird's wing tacked above the door. The hair clasp made from a razor clam. The hourglass, turned on its side—endless time, he said. Surely, that was never how he intended it. Surely he couldn't see then that the two globes of sand, separated by a narrow isthmus of glass, would prophesy a severance of two spirits, two souls. Did he know how true it would be? Indeed. The time since he left has been endless.

SIXTY

BETWEEN HIGH AND LOW TIDE, he had more than enough time. A matter of fifteen minutes and he could cast away the past, and baptized, ride the swell that would carry him to freedom. With a few gestures, well-practiced, Gilead Lodge could change his life. Or so he must have thought. I see him working it all out in his mind before he ever laid the first plank against keel or fitted oar to lock or lashed sail to mast, fashioning his means of escape, as though building one thing would give him the courage to tear down another.

I see what he must have pictured again and again, until it was no more shocking than the sight of his own face in the shaving mirror, looking forward to the day when his escape from this life to the next, one barrier island to another, would be as unremarkable as any afternoon's sail.

He would heave his gear into the dory, just one change of clothes and his bird books stuffed in his canvas sea bag. Shoving off the boat's dead weight through the familiar scrape of sand, he would feel the dory lift, running her through thigh-deep surf, and then, hands braced on the gunnels, a well-timed turn of the wrist to catapult him up and over. In one fluid thrust he would be at the tiller, the sails snapping overhead as they caught the wind. Worst case, there would be no wind, and he would elbow the oars overboard, feel them catch the current, and then leverage his escape, hardened palms measured against smooth wood, arms connecting along the length of the oars, to relearn, stroke by stroke, the sheer weight of water. I watch him haul aboard a fair measure of guilt, so burdensome that it demands his full attention lest the will to go forward, to find a reason to go on, should become atrophied like any muscle.

But then, this is my own vision of his leave-taking, the first of many. Perhaps that day he set out as guiltless as this daughter of his, embarking a lifetime later. Perhaps each saw only adventure ahead, mesmerized by how easily their shadows could outrace the waves, hearing their own cadence, A-way, A-way, like the rote form of a liturgy or the memory of a lullaby.

SIXTY-ONE

GILLY HAS GONE TO THE WINDOWSILL and picked up one of Gil's hourglasses, the only one that remains, one I overlooked the day he left for good. This is unusual, she says, turning it over, the white sand clocking down. She sets it back on the sill, and then comes over to my divan and sits, too close, each of us overshadowed by a wing of the swan. I move my knee away but she doesn't take the hint. Now Dash has come over the low back of the divan and clambered between us. He puts his head on my lap and looks up expectantly.

Gil went through a phase of hanging about the blacksmith's shop when he was about fourteen. He wasn't interested in turning cold iron into mineral fire, bending the iron into some practical shape and plunging it into water to cool, only to see it in service of hoof or soil or sea bottom. He wanted to transform matter into art, not re-make it in service of the ordinary. Even after the horseshoe's work was done and the old iron, honed down by miles, had been nailed for good luck above some door, it would be yet too weighty for Gil. A plow, too rooted in one place. Even anchor flukes, sanded sharp and thin after years of holding a ship tight against the current, they, too, bound him too close. Ornamenting some widow's flowerbed, rusting away amid the sea holly, they were too unpliable and unforgiving.

Instead of iron, then, Gil molded sand, heating the white mineral grains in the smithy's fire until the quartz thinned and flowed. Instead of the blacksmith's leather bellows, he filled his bare boyish chest, pleated with ribs, and breathed sand into glass. Whether from lack of interest or lack of skill, he only ever made one shape, oblong, pinched in the middle, rounded on each end, with one small hole he would later seal. He made dozens of these hourglasses, in love with the idea of a finite number of grains of sand held inside a clear chamber made of more of the same, sand turned crystalline. Together, with a tick of the wrist, they measured out eternity made visible.

I had seen him silhouetted in the smithy doorway, blowing his glass bubbles from the end of his iron pipe, but it wasn't until I visited his beach shanty that I saw his timepieces sifting the delicate inevitable seconds, suspended between more and less, then and now, always and never.

He cradled each of his hourglasses between two seashells whose curves would set the sand in motion. The tiniest ones were capped with coquinas. Slightly larger were the calicos, and then the bay scallops, and these trickled only minutes or half minutes. The rest counted out hours, rocking away on their quahog bases, the clamshells themselves timekeepers, their calcified arcs ringing outward, rocked into being by the lapse of waves. A precise hour was captured by manipulating the size of the glass or the fineness or coarseness of the sand. Collected higher or lower on the beach, each grain's formation took an eon, give or take an epoch here or there, and so his clocks kept earth's time, not mortal men's.

Over the years, his collection grew, and to me these silent sifting vessels were as oppressive as a room full of clocks ticking and cuckooing and chiming my life away. Perhaps I somehow knew he was counting the days until his escape just as I kept count of the moon's phases filling and emptying the night sky, synchronized with my own unfailingly accurate chronometer, that thin trickle of blood ticking down my leg.

Not so long after we were married, he made two more glasses. One he fashioned for the quarter hour, measuring out the magic minutes, one through fifteen, which meant staying or going, depending on the tide, and what else? Turning away from me, to the table by the bed, he would set the grains seething through the glass channel narrow as a rip in the offshore bar, the sand a pale rivulet in the moonlight. On the increasingly rare nights we stayed at the shanty, the beam of the lighthouse would illuminate the sand, slicing time into further bits, until daybreak snuffed it out.

How many times over the years did he contemplate his escape through that miserly gap, those fifteen minutes between tides?

Another glass he made thimble-sized, and kept it in his pocket, turning it as though he could change his luck, time slipping through his fingers, the long, solitary winter changing to spring, days spent surf fishing or walking the beach after a storm, the station running smoothly, the men well used to his command. Finally, summer, when he was mostly mine, until the hotel was built—then guests slipping through the hourglass, the names on the hotel register drizzling ink down the lined pages of the heavy leather book, people coming and going on the tide.

When the wind blew hard enough, it would set them all ticking on the shelf. What he loved was to wait until time had stopped, each half of each hourglass perfectly empty or perfectly full. Then he would fly along the narrow ledge, turning them over, turning time on like a faucet. And that's when I first discovered his genius or his madness, for each one in turn was calibrated, arranged in succession there on the shelf, timed to his speed and coordination, so that they would all, at the last, wind down together, the final grains falling as one. On witnessing this feat for the first time, I didn't know whether to laugh or to cry. Seeing his delight, perhaps I did both.

Save for this one on the windowsill, which I later came across in a trouser pocket, they are all gone back to sand now, the quartz grains mixed in with the shards of pulverized glass. The day he left for good, I set them all a-ticking, and when the last grains swept cleanly from the upper globes and the sand sat smug and stolld, stoppered, nowhere else to fall, I smashed them one by one.

SIXTY-TWO

— I'M HOPING YOU CAN EXPLAIN SOMETHING I heard my two oldest sisters conspiring about under the covers, Gilly says.

— Is that one of the questions I tore to shreds the day you arrived? I ask her.

— Actually, it is. I mean, when you hear stuff whispered, you figure it must be bad.

— No. It just means people don't have anything better to do than to stir up stories they have no business talking about.

— Well, it was about Papa, and I want to know.

— I can assure you I have better things to do.

— Like what?

— Replace the rotten siding on the boathouse.

— What for? You don't keep your boat there.

— Well I might. Anyway, go ahead. Let's get this over with.

— All right. I overheard my sisters telling how some classmates at school said that Papa was kicked out of the Life-Saving Service because he refused to go out on a rescue. Now thanks to you, I know he wasn't kicked out, he just left.

— Deserted, I say.

— Left the station, deserted his post, whatever. You said they found a letter on his desk at the station, saying he was leaving everything in good order.

— *Leaving the service forever, for reasons which I will not explain...* I suppose you could say that was a kindness, except then he went on to say any monies owed to him should come to me. As if I were an object of charity. As if I wanted his money.

Gilly sighs, fidgets. Shaking her foot, she pulls at her hair.

— I certainly don't want your sympathy, I say. And would you please hold still.

Another sigh. She tucks her feet under her and crosses her arms, but then one knee begins to jiggle. It's enough to make me seasick, if I were the type. I move to the other end of the sofa.

— The thing is, are you telling me he didn't refuse to go out? So why would my classmates say that? she asks. That's about the worst thing you could ever do. The Blue Book says you have to go out, doesn't say a damn thing about coming back. I can't believe my papa would have sat on shore and not helped somebody. My grandfather said he'd heard tell how Papa had instructed his crew to let him drown at Pollock Rip if he were washed overboard rather than risk their own lives to save him. Then my sisters go whispering that he was a coward, refusing to go out on some rescue.

— That ridiculous story followed Gil all the way to Carolina? Well let me put that to rest right this minute. I have all the facts. And I have excellent recall, especially when it comes to flat-out lies. Gil might have embarrassed himself over that girl down there, but he would never do anything to spoil his reputation in the service.

— You said he deserted.

— No, I didn't. Well, if I did, it's because you provoked me. He resigned. Technically, he resigned.

— Then why'd he change his name?

— You are being impertinent. Of course, I know where you get that from.

I see I've hurt her feelings, but I can't help who her mother is. And for once, I'm eager to answer one of her questions.

SIXTY-THREE

*THE DAY OF THE AWARDS CEREMONY was the day construction began on
the Chatham Beach Hotel. Some people say* the wreck of the *Phoenician*
was the beginning of the end of Gil's career in the Life-Saving Service.
As they like to say, that wreck is the reason he went into the business of
changing people's dirty bed linen. Others claim it was my idea, a way
to keep him home. Naturally, I disagree with both notions.

The hotel was a way to quiet the clamor that had first started
when Gil began his taxidermy, people wanting his stuffed birds in
their parlors, his services as a hunting guide, or simply the privilege
of watching him shoot. In this case, it was people wanting access to
the best hunting grounds, not for his style of hunting, in the rough,
but the gentlemanly sort of hunting, a guide doing all the work,
someone to pluck and truss and roast their birds, to pour their brandy, light their cigars, clean their guns.

— Why cater to them? I asked.

— The hunters are already here, he said. Maiming everything in
sight. Shooting on Sundays. Leaving carcasses on the beach. If they're

guests, I'll at least have a little control, can teach them something, keep them from decimating the flocks or driving the birds elsewhere. Misguided fools all summer, misguided ships all winter. I can manage them both.

In May of 1891, before the first hammer struck nail, Gil was ridiculed—no one will trek out to the beach with a wagonload of luggage, the timing of the crossing is too tricky, people are too used to staying in town—but in no time, it seemed all of Boston was ready to head this way, every room reserved. Before construction was finished, he needed to enlarge the hotel, adding wings on either side. Even the extra rooms quickly booked, before there were beds, or sheets to put on them. Suddenly there was no turning back.

There are certain events in life that shock: climbing the stairs you've trod a million times, until with one wrong step you land at the bottom with a broken neck. Other events seem so inevitable, you can feel them coming on; arthritic bones attuned to the weather, you resign yourself to a new way of being. The construction of the hotel, the wreck of the *Phoenician*, these events ached long before they began, long after they were over.

An awards ceremony to celebrate the rescue of the *Phoenician* was announced. Gil was not one to begrudge those civilians their Silver Life-Saving Medals. Never mind that their soft, idle hands were more used to putting tins on the grocery shelf or playing cards in the back room of the store. It's a fact, they did indeed leap up out of their chairs racked back on the porch, and they hauled to it, and risked their lives to save others, or else why would Gil have put their names forward for such a rare honor?

If they deserved a medal, and no one says they didn't, what of Gil's men? They were the ones who, day after day, veered between intense boredom and the screaming onrush of terror. They were the ones who waited an hour or more for their fingers to unmake the shape of an oar, tense with clutching or freezing or fear. It was they who kept hearing the crack of a mast or a windborne scream, or a sound more immediate, their own teeth chattering. They heard in their sleep the bitten-off curse, the sleet sizzling in their beards. They dreamed the unrestful dream of some poor soul's last exhalation, hot breath leaving a cold body that soon would be colder still. While others sat drinking coffee around the stove of a morning, his men had to swim, to row, to rig. By turns they might be called to serve as doctor, confessor, reader of last rites, undertaker, bearer of bad news.

This they feared daily, that somewhere out on the sea, off Pollock Rip or on Chatham Bar, there would be those who could not be saved. But in fact, during Gil's tenure, there were only three. Three hundred seventy-nine lives imperiled, three hundred seventy-seven lives saved: the one man lost overboard at midnight more than twenty-five miles distant from the station, the other who was as good as dead, suffocated from lime gas by the time Gil transferred him into the surfboat. And then there was the babe: lost at sea. Not added in the count.

SIXTY-FOUR

AFTER THE RECEPTION honoring the townspeople's heroism, I do not go straight home, carrying my empty crystal dish. Instead, I take a meandering walk that somehow manages to include four streets, each with very different houses, different residents. No one is home. Of course, my esteemed former citizens are still rummaging through the soggy remnants of dishes now so commingled that a dab of Boston baked beans sits scrofulous and brown amid the pale chunks of escalloped potatoes. Still chewing over the story of the rescue, they work the details like a piece of gristle, which grows ever larger in their mouths.

I walk along Mullet Lane, sand seeping through the lace-holes of my kid boots. The hem of my dress is one hue paler than navy as it collects dust along the path, this part of town too poor for crushed oyster shells. The houses here are nearly as ramshackle as those in Scrabbletown, careening in the direction of the prevailing wind. Here a board never felt the sweep of a laden paintbrush; there a batten bears the fine carving of someone else's eave, the white paint barely flaking. Crate slats pockmarked with nails, a broken mast, a ship's hatch, all combine in a marvelous mishmash resigned to be less than the sum of its parts, a less exuberant version of Gil's Folly. Such is the home of the silver medalist Thaddeus Andrews.

By now, loose-limbed with drink, he will be as leeward as his house, and when he staggers home, I picture him tumbling into a bed whose ropes have not been tightened nor its ticking turned, the eelgrass stuffing flat and sour with sweat. The medal will fall out of his clenched fist, and it will be hours or days before he will think to look for it, shining feebly on the bare sanded floorboards. When he discovers it, he will run his fingers over the letters engraved in the medal to trace their shapes, and since he has memorized the words, he can now claim to read. His hands themselves are a book, each scar, each layer of hard callus a chapter no one has bothered to recite.

But for now, he will fall into bed, his knit fisherman's cap pulled down over his reddish-blond curls. He lives alone, although some say he has a Portuguese wife in Gloucester. I picture her a dark beauty named Consuela and I see him place his silver medal in his sea chest along with a ribbon from her hair. The medal, engraved with the image of a man struggling in a heavy sea and a woman offering one end of a long scarf, will remind him of Consuela on occasion, but neither will much change his life.

Thad is popular at the store, not out front by the stove or on the porch, but in the back room, where a card game is an easy way to take a drunk man's money. Perhaps every third or fourth hand he will appear sober, and then he's unbeatable, with luck and an uncanny knack for counting cards. Given what they take off him the other nights, it all evens out, from the other players' point of view. After all, they've saved him a trip to Gloucester. Here, he can lose a week's pay without ever leaving home.

Not far from Thad Andrews's house live Joseph and Polly Lucas. Their house is also made from salvage, but since Joe is a wrecker, he's had first pick of what's washed ashore or been lightered in from ships run aground on the bar. What he doesn't use, he sells, but from the piles of goods heaped in the yard, it seems he has plans for most everything.

At the awards ceremony, one would hardly recognize Joe. His clothes are clean and neatly pressed. For once, his wife has done for him what she does for others all day long: washing, mending, ironing clothes for those citizens of Chatham who've cut back on servants' employ. Otherwise, he goes about with clothes salty as a Smithfield ham, coated with a thick layer of grime.

Joe spends most of his free time at the store, sometimes helping to stock shelves, but mostly contemplating his next jump. In winter by the stove, in summer on the porch, he plays checkers for hours. He eats salt cod like candy while his big hand hovers over the board. His checkers are so grimy no one will play with them.

What will Joe do with his medal? I expect Polly will make a lovely velvet cushion, stealing a bit of cloth from someone's hem, thinking it will never be missed, just as no one has ever missed the other rectangles, squares, triangles, and circles she's snipped from their laundry, enough to make a quilt where each bit represents not a particular dress or pair of trousers, but a remembered slight or word ill spoken by the wearer, so that each night Joe and Polly sleep beneath a seething discontent. I once saw the quilt airing out on a lilac bush one late spring morning. Gil's brass button, with its insignia of a life buoy crossed and interlocked with an oar and a boat hook and the letters USLSS, which had gone missing from his blue kersey uniform, was set in a circle cut from one of my patterned summer gowns. It was the last time our clothes were laundered by her jealous hands. Just so, Joe's medal will sit smug in the center of filched velvet, like a hot brand stamped into tender flesh saying *Mine and not yours.*

A few blocks away from Joe Lucas's house is Samuel Rowe's mercantile establishment, where the rescuers were rallied to action. It stands on Water Street, not far from the pilot boats, the boats that in turn were not far from the ship foundered on the bar.

The store is shut for the day since there's no one about to buy the tinned peaches or the Irish potatoes, the buttons or bolts of cloth, the waders or oilskins that hang disembodied from the rafters. Nor is anyone at his home next door. Sam Rowe is a widower, and given how much time he spends at the store, most people call it an extravagance that he keeps house at all.

His wide rump planted, the stool swiveling so he seldom needs to stand, Sam could devise an entire life's story from any one purchase. This one drank too much and thereby lost not one but two lady loves. That one has a colicky baby, her first and, she swears, her last. Another is careless with his gear and will never make any money at fishing, and yet another walks slew-footed and buys boot heels by the dozen. With each customer's purchase rung on the register or penciled into the account book, depending on his or her creditworthiness, Sam makes it his business to share what he's surmised with the next customer in line.

Samuel Rowe is not plumped on his stool behind the brass-keyed register, his boots stirruped on its rungs. He is not waving his pipe, quieting the checker players so he can hear the brassy melody of money. He, be-medaled, is still at the ceremony.

It was Sam who took the lead, gathered a crew, and commandeered the pilot boat, all the while castigating Gil and his crew for what he called their dereliction of duty. Sam was down on the wharf when the ship's crew sent up a flare, and so surely he must have known there'd be no way anyone on watch at the Chatham Beach Station could have seen it, the ship lying well north of the town, thick fog drawn like a curtain over the station to the south.

While the other men clearly loved the attention they received at the ceremony, it would be Sam who would make the rounds for years after, talking to church groups and clubs, telling of the wreck and rescue and showing off his medal. He would have a case made for his medal, although it would live outside the walnut and glass box as often as in it. At weddings and funerals and graduations it would sit on his chest, fat with pride. During his talks, he would unpin it and let it be passed around the room, and if anyone came to visit, he would rub the case as though it were a lamp, the medal a genie who had granted his one wish of fame. But there are all kinds of fame, and although none would call him this to his face, his nickname would become Medal Sam, pronounced *Meddlesome*, an apt name for the town's busybody.

Last of the rescuers is Cyrus Collins. My walk takes me out of the way in order to pass by the house of Cyrus and Nell, down by the old saltworks, just past the windmill. For years, Cyrus had gone to sea, and each year upon his return, there'd be a new babe in arms to greet him, one for each of his ten voyages, along with a spare, twins born one year a nice bonus. When an anchor chain snapped and broke his leg, that was the end of his voyaging, and for some reason, the end of his wife's pregnancies, as though the children were not his but the offspring of whales. No more whales, no more children.

While Nell and the children work the bogs or bale salt hay or help out at sheep-shearing time, Old Man Cyrus spends his days sitting with his bad leg stretched out for Sam Rowe's customers to trip over as they select their goods. To make up for his stiff leg, his arms have the strength of ten men, and he earns extra money loading blocks of ice cut from Little Mill Pond or shoveling sawdust in the icehouse. He is likeable, with a lovely singing voice and a way with riddles and yarns.

As for his children, even though he ruffles the heads of all of his shock-haired boys and pulls the plaits of his innumerable girls, no one has ever heard him call any of them by name. Most likely, it's because, named as they are for ports of call, ships, and captains, while each voyage is vivid and he can recount each whale, its girth and length, the children all run together so that this girl Polynesia and that girl the *Portia*, this boy Samoa and that boy the *Roark* are one and the same, alike as four globes, all spinning blue. And there are seven more besides.

I've often thought that Cyrus and Nell have so many children, weeks might go by before they would miss one, and if they did, perhaps it would be a relief, with one less haircut to give or plait to braid, one less fish to clean or potato to peel for supper.

As I walk by the house, I see all the children are home, although they are as hard to count as schooling fish. Two little girls sit in a huddle, sailing dead leaves in the rainwater collected in the old wooden sluice that once funneled briny water to the saltworks. One boy is hanging from a rope tied to the vane of the windmill while his brothers catch at his ankles as he slowly spins up and out of reach. An older boy stands to the side, taking bets on which child will be the last to drop to the ground, with heavy odds on whether a leg will be broken. This one always has money in his pockets, and this habit alone is sufficient to stir talk that Sam Rowe and not Cyrus is his father.

With their parents at the awards ceremony, one would think the eldest would be minding them, but she sits oblivious in the shade of the dogtrot between house and kitchen, mending a pile of clothes. Cyrus copied the design, if such a ramshackle affair could be said to have a design, from a house down south in Charleston, he said.

The littlest, a boy of about four, reminds me of Gil with his unruly black hair. His name is Fiji, and he smiles shyly when he sees me walking by. As for the rest of the children, they pay no mind, intent on their games.

I feel certain the Life-Saving Medal will have a place of honor in this swarming beehive of a house for no more than a day. It will be tossed, spun, hidden, a silver plaything to be lost and found and lost again in Cyrus's sea chest overflowing with useless treasure. Here

I imagine half a coconut hull with a bit of dried meat still clinging, a sailor's valentine with some of its delicate shells broken or missing, bits of coral and glass beads, a japanned box, a deck prism, all intermixed with a jumble of rope contorted into carrick bends and stopper knots, savoys and sheepshanks and Josephines, sailor's knots once nicely framed and labeled but now unraveling in a heap.

The medal will be fought over like the shrunken head from West Africa or the monkey's paw from Papua New Guinea, which the boys most prize. As for the girls, their favorite is undoubtedly the bisque doll's head, the doll once the star of their puppet shows until she was beheaded with a real, true, cross-my-heart-and-hope-to-die pirate's sword wielded during a sneak attack by the boys.

No one knows what happened to the doll's body. The brothers claimed a wild tribe of doll cannibals ate her. As a result, one of the girls fashioned a wimple for her bodyless head since she surely must have been a missionary, although her sisters were divided on whether she had actually been a missionary and whether missionaries wore wimples. Some claimed she was Theodosia Burr, made to walk the plank by pirates off the coast of Hatteras. No, the boys said, else how could she have walked the plank with no head? Ah, it was her ghost, said the girls. And so they entertained themselves for days.

Now that the family's circumstances are reduced, and these prizes have been worn down by time's incessant fingering, perhaps I'll buy Fiji Collins a toy boat in place of the broken ship's model he's pretending to sail across the waves of sand he's swept up into peaks, perilous as any sea.

This is one house, then, where the medal will be warmly cherished for itself, not for some aggrandized heroics. Fiji's brothers and sisters will give in when he reaches up for it, for after all, he's the littlest, and his sweet fingers will lovingly trace the shiny silver contours as he falls asleep with it under his pillow tonight.

SIXTY-FIVE

THE CEREMONY TO COMMEMORATE the rescue of the crew of the Phoenician *had been absent one person, though Gil could claim he was on duty at the station and therefore* unable to attend. The truth was, from the time the lumber wagon left the sawmill everyone knew he had one foot out the door, ready to embark on another career, even as he kept on with his duties.

I had no such excuse. I went.

I was pleasant to everyone, congratulating the men and their wives, their mothers, their children, their great-aunts, their step-cousins, the men who hung about the store too young or too old to help with the rescue that day, Old Doc Martin who brought three of the four silver medalists into the world. I looked each of them in the eye as I shook his or her hand. "The men did a fine thing." Or "Captain Lodge and I offer our sincere congratulations."

It certainly was a heroic rescue. Aren't they all, more or less? But even if Gil never said so, I believe he surely must have felt it was only due to their civilian status that they were awarded the second highest honor in the US Life-Saving Service, and that otherwise, they would not have been recognized. After all, his own men, season after season, performed rescues in equally or even more dangerous circumstances.

Never mind his own heroism, swimming out to Captain Best's sloop. Gil deserved the gold for that rescue. He never talked about it, and if I brought it up, he would get up and leave the room.

I sat politely and listened to the speeches, and afterward stood eating the food I had helped prepare, hearing the comments ill-concealed behind hands or said outright. I kept an agreeable smile on my face and heard for the second or fifth time how a squall came out of the north-northeast, how Sam Rowe organized the men hanging about his store, their first pot of coffee only half-brewed, how they launched one of the town's pilot boats and headed for the cut-through.

I heard how a vessel, a ship, a schooner, a two-masted schooner, a schooner whose sails were shredded, whose canvas sheets were frozen ribbons, how it creaked and groaned as the tattered sails and unte-thered rigging lashed the men clinging to the main peak halyards, to the wheelhouse, to the masts, take your pick. How the vessel was wrecked, was bilged, was hard aground on the Outer Bar. I heard how Sam called for volunteers, how four, twenty, fifty, how a dozen stepped forward, the only definite number, four, the four men on the platform, the four silver medals depending from blue-and-white striped ribbons, four chests proudly plumped, such courage on display for all to see.

Over cod cakes I heard how Joe Lucas pushed at the stern post, water reaching his armpits, last man aboard, as though he were the first man ever to shove into a December sea. I heard, over oyster stew, how the boat capsized, how despite how hard Thaddeus Andrews struggled at the sweep, the wave crested too soon so that men, oars, and boat were thrown back upon the shore, although not in that particular order, if anyone was paying attention.

The clams were tasteless. More so than usual, they defied chewing, growing larger in my mouth as I listened to how the boat's larboard was split and the men stood shivering while others fetched a second boat. Chewing, chewing, water again to the armpits, chewing as they slid over the crest and down the back of the wave, the boat broached, the boat pitch-poling, the men leaping clear, the boat driven high on the beach, a heap of splintered planking and ribs, fit only for kindling. I chewed, thinking all the boys in town would be fighting over splinters, just to say they had a souvenir from the Silver Medal Wreck, as they were already beginning to call it.

We had now reached the cranberry salad stage of the tale, where the fearless men had to wait for not four, not seven, but eleven waves until the timing was right to launch the third rescue boat. By now, I couldn't stomach another bite, as I heard how in an hour they barely made two hundred yards, thinking of a whole fleet, a whole navy of wrecks that over these past years Gil and his men had crawled toward.

A cross-sea rose up beneath the starboard bow, the men intoned, as though they were describing each inning, play by play, of some interminable game of baseball, how Thad Andrews held the bat, the mighty crack, home run! They had crossed the Northeast Bar. Before them now lay the open Atlantic.

I walked over to the dessert table while the men rowed dead to windward, positioning themselves to ride the sea back in, close enough to the schooner to allow the wrecked sailors to jump for it. The boat rode the crest of a wave, both the oars and the sweep beating air. They shot forward, coming alongside the schooner. Joe and Thad stood up to help steer, hurrah, poling their oars down, seeking water as the breaking sea sheared away. "Port oar! Port oar!" Cyrus Collins yelled, and the crowd moved their forks in unison to the left side of their plates, as Cy told how they rode so high they feared they would shoot clear over the schooner, between her two masts. The boat swept past, the sailors clinging to the halyards as though stunned, Rowe and his men stunned, too, at the thought they would have to do it all over again. "Aye, again!" they shouted agreement, and the crowd cheered, "Aye, again!"

Back across the Outer Bar they went, back out into the open Atlantic, lining the boat up to ride an incoming breaker. As they approached the vessel, everyone knew it was the last chance. "Jump for your lives, you fools, save yourselves!"

Over by the apple pie, I had already heard the story's ending. A second time, and I might regurgitate my dinner. I slipped away, knowing that this story, these stories, were already multiplying, mutating, until the real events of that day would bear no more resemblance than a bluebird does a buzzard, never mind that they both hatch out from an egg.

The rescue was still being written about long after Gil was dead. I doubt many had bothered to read the official record in the Life-Saving Service's annual report, so most people believed whatever the press chose to print. You would think someone might notice, however, that in one sensationalized account the sailors dropped into the sea, one by one, in balletic slow motion. In another, four of the crew landed in the boat all in a heap into the stern sheets, with brave Cyrus Collins holding the pintle of the oar in one hand while hauling the shipwrecked captain over the gunnel, steering with one hand while with the other, he lifted the man above his head like a barbell.

That day in 1891, the day four men who usually spent their time hanging about the store got the medals Gil and his men deserved ten times over, I heard the snickers, how by the time high and mighty Captain Gilead Lodge came aboard, she was empty of all save her heavy load of coal, all the hard work done, the sea slick calm. I heard the whispers, Cap'n Lodge saw the flare same as them boys, sure, he just didn't want to go, should be dismissed from the Service, locked up in jail for dereliction of duty, didn't go, went but got there too late, don't know which is worse. Heard the accusations of bias, the

official account in the USLSS Annual Report written by who else but
the keeper of the station himself: Capt. Gil Lodge.

I kept walking, the crowd parting before me. *Here, don't forget
your bowl. Why, Mrs. Lodge, everyone says you make the best cranberry
salad, see, your bowl is clean as a baby's bottom.* I took the dish and the
sideways comment without acknowledgment and walked on.

This is a fickle coast, with inlets opening and closing, what was
shoal water one day turned to channels swift and deep the next,
Nauset Beach slowly rolling over itself, a behemoth of sand moving southerly and westerly, even without storms as battering rams.
Within a year after she foundered on the bar, the *Phoenician* forsook
the sea and began sailing the sands, the tides burying and resurrect-
ing her broken hull on the beach, moving her south, to within only
a few hundred yards of the life-saving station. It would seem even
Neptune conspired to perpetuate the claim that Gil refused to go
out. Every freckled schoolboy, every parasol-shaded church woman
saw the wreck within a stone's throw of the station, all the proof they
needed that Gil and his men sat cozy inside while townspeople risked
their lives to rescue the sailors.

Never mind that when the schooner foundered, she was well
north of the station, the weather so thick that all the man on watch
could make out was a flare in the distance that might have just been
a bonfire up the beach. Even so, they launched the surfboat, made
their way north, and arrived on board at seven in the morning, two
hours after she'd foundered, only to find the vessel empty of all save
her cargo.

So it was left to Gil and his men to salvage her load of coal in a
snowstorm. If they felt like naughty children who, instead of walnuts
and oranges, found a lump of coal in their Christmas stockings, well,
they never said.

SIXTY-SIX

EACH MORNING, GIL SET THE CREW AT THEIR DRILLS, and if they felt the lack of something silver pinned to their chests, they kept it to themselves, launching the surfboat with vigor, practicing swamping her so she could be righted, or firing the Lyle gun and listening to the line sing as it flew out of the faking box. Gil never showed he minded either, but I could tell by his walk, the way he held his dark head, how he closed his lids halfway, looking neither here nor there, that something had gone out of him. Whether it was this, or my so-called ambition for him, the hotel's beginnings marked the end of something.

He would walk the few hundred yards from the station to the hotel site, where trusses arched like whale ribs, overwhelming the sky. By mid-afternoon, more than a dozen hammers were making a rapid-fire din that drowned out the sound of the ocean as a crew of carpenters sheathed the walls in record time. At sunset, all the men had piled into three boats, heading back to town, except for two perched in the rafters, hammering at shingles on the cupola roof like a pair of gulls picking the last shreds of blubber from a rack of bones. Gil stopped and lifted his head as though a stench were rising from the hot sand, but there was no rotting carcass in sight, only the hotel, as out of place as a leviathan hulked up on dry land.

I had told him he could give up the enterprise, but he said no. Before the first nail was driven, we had more reservations than rooms. All the initial speculation in the *Monitor* about the folly of building a hotel on the beach—Gil's Folly Number Two—was soon put to rest.

At the station, the day's drills finished, the crew might have tried to talk him into a contest, who could coil a hank of rope around the wooden pegs of the faking box in the shortest time. It was a contest Gil always won and therefore seldom played. On this day would he have felt the need to win at something? Beating the clock was better than taking his men's money at poker, so it may be that he lined up his box alongside three other men's. As the rope flew through his fingers, it must have all seemed pointless. He threw the heavy line into the box and walked off to spend that night, as he did more and more often, at the shanty, with only his birds for company.

SIXTY-SEVEN

— I NEVER EVEN KNEW HE HAD A HOTEL HERE in Chatham, Gilly says. Don't you think it's strange that my father would just up and move to North Carolina, and start the same life all over again?

— Right. Just one more thing you don't know.

— Not fair. That's why I came. To find out. But it kind of makes me feel good, to know he had a successful hotel here as well as our own Tranquil House.

— I am really not in the mood, I say. All this is stirring up things I'd just as soon forget. I've had enough of you for one day. Go get a haircut or something. Get out from under my feet.

— Like what? Stirring up what?

— Didn't I just say they were things I'd just as soon forget?

Of course, she doesn't leave, even when I get in the hammock and pull a hat over my face. She sits in the chair, pushing the hammock with her foot.

— Stop. You'll make me sick. Besides bruising me all over. If anyone were to see me, they'd arrest you for assault and battery.

— You're always exaggerating, she says.

— I embellish, not exaggerate. There's a difference. So. Shall I embellish upon the story of the hotel?

Gilly plucks the hat from my face. I take that as a yes.

Old Man Nicholson made it his business to explain it all to me several years after Gil left for the last time. I was on the beach, nailing down gull wings on the shanty's roof, chinking the walls with eelgrass, trying to hold together what was left of Gil's Folly. Wind and tide seemed determined to pluck down or wash over my last best place of solace.

The old man had been a wrecker on Monomoy and had done some long-lining for swords and halibut with Gil's grandfather. We were fond of each other in a standoffish kind of way. He was always ready to peck my cheek. I was always ready to turn it away.

He poked his head through the whale-socket window I had opened to air out the shanty. I smelled his pipe before I heard his chronic cough, like the bark of a seal, a single short bark that always made me laugh, or at least it did back when I still knew how to laugh.

I came out of the shanty; the air was colder inside than out, as it often is in spring. We sat on the driftwood bench and looked at the sea.

— I been thinking, missy, he says. Wondering, like.

I continued to watch the sea, the breakers politely tucking their chins. He turned his head to look at me, tapped his pipe against the heel of his hand.

— Yes'm been doing some pondering. Seen that brochure he done had printed here—don't they have printing presses down there in Carolina? Weren't snooping, now, Mr. Dunn hires me on occasion to empty his bins. One dropped to the floor, I didn't go digging for it. Did stick my hand in to look at the funeral program for old Barnett Stockton, see what lies they was telling about him dead that hadn't already been told about him alive.

— Like I was saying, picked that nice hotel brochure up'n off the floor, was going to give it to you, no harm in giving you an extra copy or two, a nice job, green borders, photographs, that family shield or whatever with the Latin on it, the Lodges always did know how to promote a business, when I saw the name. 'Tweren't the Chatham Beach Hotel, 'twas the Hotel Roanoke.

— Hmmm, where is that, I asked myself? Didn't know of no new hotels hereabouts. Didn't know you had expanded your enterprise with a sister hotel with a matching brochure.

— Well since it were laying there and since I were going to give it to you, free like, I thought to myself, may as well look it over, that way I could speak to you right smartly about it, a compliment easy to hand is always a good thing, I tells myself.

— Then what do I see but *Capt. Gilead Lodge, Proprietor, Hotel Roanoke, Manteo NC* there on the back. The brochure is proclaiming the famous-like hunting grounds, don't that sound like your own piece about Chatham Beach? And the wonderful hospitality, the bounteous fare, the peckable, is that right, the peckable service?

— Impeccable, I say. Another wave politely tucks under, prim as a Sunday school teacher, no knowing what undertow is at play there.

— Peckable, yes ma'am. So I take that sucker, and I tear it right in two, yes I do. And put it back in the bin, way down at the bottom. The whole time I'm sweeping the floor, I'm thinking to myself, why would a man go to all the trouble to pull up stakes, go way down yonder, and turn around and do it all again. The whole shooting match. Hooks up with them life-savers for awhile, builds a shanty and goes barefoot as Crusoe without the benefit of Friday. Then ups and marries, moves one island over, and builds himself another nigh-on identical hotel, serving up the same fare, taking the same damn Yankees shooting the same damn birds, pardon my language. Bet the man can't even come up with a different name for his next dog. Least the name of his next hotel, after the Chatham Beach and the Roanoke, was somewhat original, Tranquility, was it? The one thing

I do know, without even looking, is this here Cape Cod wife is a whole sight prettier than the one down there, even if that new one is younger.

He barked, tamped his pipe, reached over, patted my hand, tried to hold it. I slipped it out from under his. Another wave dipped its chin. So unoriginal, that ocean.

— So I keep thinking on it, he says. And the best I can figure, 'tweren't none of my business now but I think of myself as a student of the menses and the womenses, so I'm supposing that maybe one day a man is walking down the beach and lightning strikes, so close that the damp sand sizzles, like water hitting a hot skillet. His feet get blistered. The hair on his head gets singed. It comes just shy of killing him.

— Now this does something to him. He messes about, can't get settled, always checking the sky for storm clouds. Hell, he's so spooked he even gets in the wardrobe behind the clothes when he hears the least rumble of thunder.

— Meanwhile, plenty of storms come and go. Nothing happens. He gets rained on, hailed on, sleeted, snowed on. Lightning bolts strike, far out to sea, he sees heat lightning skitter sideways across the sky. He don't get in the back of the wardrobe no more, don't even check the barometer much to speak of. He finally reckons he's safe.

— But all the same, he's done disrupted his whole life, hiding out from that lightning. So he rebuilds exactly the same life, keeps to the same routine, right down to the number of times he runs a comb through his hair. Course the Cap's hair was so thick, that was mighty hard to do, but you know what I mean.

— So best I can figure, one day lightning strikes. And then no more lightning strikes. Maybe that's all there is to it.

He looked at me as if to say, now I know Gil Lodge didn't get struck by no lightning bolt, so what the hell was it?

I continued to sit, watching the waves tuck and roll. After a while, he got up, patted my shoulder, and walked off down the beach. I heard him bark, quick and sharp, shaking his head.

All I can think of is Gil. The French call love at first sight a *coup de foudre*, a stroke of lighting. It leaps from cloud to cloud, impossible to say where it will go to ground, pointless to count the seconds between thunder and lightning, one mile per second, counting the seconds, one hundred and one, one hundred and two, how close is it, how long does it take, love found, only to lose it?

The old man was wrong. There was a bolt, and it found me, an unwitting lightning rod. That same frisson of electric current branched and forked, found Gil, struck him to his core, the same joy turned to sorrow blasting us both. Like a single tree, split asunder, we fell in opposite directions. I would that we had been sand-struck, become fulgurite, a heap of molten sand fused into a single twisted branch of glass formed by the same current, that our sadness might have brought us together instead of sending us helter-skelter, forever running for cover.

SIXTY-EIGHT

FIJI WAS A MISUNDERSTANDING. True, I had no business that took me down to the old saltworks. It had only been a week since I'd walked that way carrying my dirty dish from the ceremony. But who hasn't gone for a ramble on a day seemingly made for window gazing, until the sun shining through a leaf, just so, catches your eye and calls you out. Who hasn't strayed, following the map laid down by a monarch's hectic wingbeats. Then it's hopeless. The scent of a lilac waylays you. A bird hops from twig to branch to fence picket, and the next thing you know, you're three streets, or six, from where you started.

As usual, there were no adults in sight, Cyrus Collins most likely at Rowe's Mercantile, his wife, Nell, and her two oldest helping with the lambing over at the Gould farm. The other nine, all home.

A Saturday, so no school, but there were enough children in this family to populate a schoolyard, and that's what the beaten-down ground around their house loosely resembled. Using an old keg and a length of board, two were seesawing. One child tried to bathe a terrier, which paddled in circles in a huge rusted try-pot once used to render whale oil from blubber. Two girls turned a jump rope, a third poised, bobbing her head, waiting for just the right time to run in. Two others were playing hopscotch, tossing shells to mark their next jump onto the squares scratched out in the dirt with a bit of whale-bone. And Fiji, backed up against a silver poplar that had seeded itself just inside the fence, sat drawing a picture on a chalkboard. He appeared to be about the size our twins would have been by now, a bit tall for his age, lanky, with uncooperative hair.

I leaned over the snaggle-toothed pickets and asked the boy what he was sketching.

— A whale, miss.

He held the chalkboard up at a slant for me to see. The flukes and humped back were nicely shaded. The eye had a malevolent gleam, skillfully drawn with a fleck of white in the black orb.

— Where are the harpooners? I asked.

— Oh, no, miss, they mustn't go after this one. This one's a killer. Moby-Dick.

— What a smart boy you are to be, what, just four?

— Nearly five.

Four fingers outstretched, he wiggled his thumb in and out.

— And how is it you know of Moby-Dick? I asked.

— My pap knew an old sailor what served aboard the *Essex*. The ship what was rammed by the real Moby-Dick.

— I have a book about the white whale, with beautiful pictures, I told him. Would you like to see it?

— Yes, ma'am, I would. I just have to ask the Portia.

At Fiji's approach, his sister abruptly dropped her twin brother, the Roark, as she dismounted from the seesaw.

Eleven years ago, Cyrus had left on the *Portia*, was shipwrecked in the Falklands, and picked up by the *Roark*, so neither Cyrus nor his wife was surprised when twins arrived. Everyone ran the two words together as if they were spelled *Theportia* and *Theroark*. Their profiles were so striking they could have been identical figureheads on their respective namesakes.

A tabby cat followed the Portia, winding in and out of the broken slats in the fence, then rubbed itself against the girl's legs.

— This lady has a real picture of the white whale. Can I please go see it?

— You'll just give yourself more nightmares. You need to quit thinking about that old whale, the Portia said.

— No, I won't get a nightmare. Please? She said she'd give me paper and pen so I can be a proper artist. I told her with this chalkboard somebody's always erasing my pictures.

— You're the keeper's wife, ma'am? What lives down by the bluff?

— Yes, I answered. I won't keep him long. We'll have a nice visit, maybe some cake.

At that, I was swarmed with children, but I told them perhaps another time, this is Fiji's turn to visit. I felt no particular qualms about lying.

— Aw, it's 'cause you're the baby, shouted one of the boys.

— Don't worry, Fiji said sweetly. If I'm good, maybe this miss will let me bring some cake home to you to share.

I would bake a cake for each of them, all eleven of them, if it would make him happy. I don't bake. For him, I would have learned.

SIXTY-NINE

As we walked home, Fiji stopped to show me a willow with a rotten stump where he kept two quartz stones he'd found on the beach. In the dim light, the willow branches flowed and pooled like a waterfall, no barren waters of Babylon here, with little Fiji next to me. He struck the stones together and then held out his cupped hands for me to see. The white rocks glowed, their inner fire refracting the rosy flesh of his fingers.

He was full of stories, the escapades of Samoa and Polynesia and his other siblings, their schoolyard adventures, tales of his father's whaling voyages. He did not speak of his mother, which made me glad. He would stop on the path and put his hand on my wrist when he got to an exciting part, saying, *And then Miss Captain Lodge, and then and then*, like a dream unspooling.

— You have very nice manners, Fiji, but you don't have to call me miss. You can call me Mimi, I said.

On he chattered, *Mimi this, Mimi that*, as if I had meant all along to adopt the name I called my mother during our short life together. It didn't seem out of place, on this day, with this boy.

We sat on the porch in the swing. When it slowed, he would clamber down, run behind and give it a mighty push, then dodging between the swing and the porch rail, come back around, timing his leap back up into my lap. He grew quiet looking at Taber's illustrations in Melville's book, his small finger tracing the lines. I gave him a glass of milk and a piece of Gil's favorite shortbread. That's when he noticed my tatted things. I showed him my whalebone shuttle, how to make picots and Josephine knots.

— There's Josephines and savoys and stopper knots that my pa tied for us where we keep our things in his sea chest, he said. And, he whispered dramatically, widening his blue eyes that reminded me of Gil's, there's a real live dead monkey's paw!

My fish were his favorite. He held one, making it swim through the air.

— It looks like a fish. It smells like a fish. But it's lacy, like a fish wearing a doll's dress. Who ever heard of such!

— There's a real flounder inside, I said, pulling apart some of the threads so he could see a bit of the dried tail, the spotted topside and pale bottom showing through.

Fiji ran his finger around the flounder's lace orb, so he could feel the second eye that migrates to the flatfish's topside.

— If I lay on my belly long enough, and hold really still, will my eyes move to the other side of my head?

— What, you don't have any eyes back there? I asked, rubbing the stubborn hair that bristled like a horse's cropped mane, uncrushable, like Gil's.

I gave him some paper and pen and ink, and he spent time drawing something large and round, which he said was Moby's eye, which made me think of Gil's whalespout chimney and socketed windows, and the next thing you knew we were down by the roses, then along the cliff path, our timing just right, across the ford before the tide turned. We chased birds down the beach and splashed in the surf, Fiji shouting, *Mimi, come look, Mimi, watch me.*

Of course, since we'd walked over, I knew there was no way back, not until the next low tide, but that was a hard thing, a fact, and this was a dream, where only what I wished to see would appear before me.

Fiji was delighted with the shanty, and ran all around it, probing each bone and timber and wing. At first he would not believe the windows were made from the sockets of a sperm whale's eyes.

— Oh, no, Mimi, a whale's eyes are big, big around as…

He looked up and down the empty beach for something to match the immensity of a whale, and pointed to the moon rising full up out of the sea, focusing its white gaze on the humpbacked waves.

— …a whale's eyes are as big as the moon!

Gil had wanted to see what a whale sees. How much more wonderful to see the world through the eyes of a boy.

We went inside and stretched out on the oriental rug, taking stock of the shells we'd collected. Gil must have been here recently, for there was a fresh cushion of eelgrass beneath the carpet. I lit an oil lamp and told Fiji how a whale is a creature of both fire and water. He swims across oceans carrying enough oil to light ten thousand lamps for ten thousand nights. We renamed his whale Aladdin. He would keep the dark away. No more nightmares about Moby-Dick.

I held the lamp high so he could see all Gil's birds, and although it was the light and shadow that flared and dipped, it was no trouble to imagine the birds shifting about on their shelf, poised for flight. He wanted to hold one, but I told him he would have to ask Gil, even if he was the specially appointed keeper of the monkey's paw this week.

I helped Fiji up onto the big bed, where he gazed up at the sweeping wings of the swan. I tucked him in and thought what to recite. Gil's rhyme.

One, two,
Three, four, five,
Once I caught a fish alive,
Six, seven,
Eight, nine, ten,
Then I let it go again.
Why did you let it go?
Because it bit my finger so.
Which finger did it bite?
This little finger on the right.

He made me recite it again, and we pretended to gobble each other's fingers like hungry fish. This one I would not let go.

I blew out the lamp and kissed Fiji goodnight. We settled in, the moon and the lighthouse beam giving just enough illumination for me to see Fiji's small shape beneath the feather comforter. The swan hovered above us like a watchful angel.

I was nearly asleep when Gil came through the door.

SEVENTY

THE OCEAN IS RUNNING HEADLONG AT THE BEACH. I well know the feeling. If the impetus for each wave is some three thousand miles to the east, or farther, three hundred thousand miles to the moon, what is it that impels longing, and can the thing longed for and the longing itself ever be separated? Like a single wave could be parted from the pure energy driving it shoreward.

— Are you going to tell me or not?

— Tell you what?

—What happened, Gilly says.

— To the hotel? It was moved back from the sea a few times. Eventually it was razed. The lumber was sold at auction. Knock on any number of front doors in Chatham and you'll be knocking on what was once a door opening into one of the hotel's guestrooms.

— No, I mean to Fiji.

— Well, what do you think happened. Gil took him home that night.

The tilt of the head, one brow raised, the other narrowing, the tug at her hair, it could be Gil sitting there. Like her father, she says nothing. No words needed when the body is such an eloquent spokesman.

— You came all this way to find out about your father. You didn't know one thing about Fiji Collins before you got here. So try to stay on the subject, please. I'm sorry I mentioned him. Your father built a hotel, the first one on the beach. And we ran it. Together.

— You know, I can't really picture you running a hotel.

The ocean is still surging. The hammock is not swinging. She's no use, can't be relied on for the simplest thing. I reach for Dash's tail and pull, using his weight as traction to set the hammock moving again. We got along fine without her, we'll get along fine when she's gone.

— Excuse me, but I can do anything I put my mind to, I say.

—I'm sure you can. And hotel keeping is one thing I can't see your mind getting anywhere near.

Honestly, sometimes I do have to laugh at her.

The guns were oiled and seated in their mahogany racks, boxes of birdshot filled the gun-cabinet drawer, linens and dishes had made the trip from town at high tide. Sheets and pillowcases and hand towels were cushioned between stacks of plates and saucers and wrapped around tea cups and brandy snifters and shot glasses. Both linens and dishes had to be washed again, having been soaked by a wave in the crossing. At last, in the summer of 1891, we were open for business, but it was more of the same. If there's one thing I dislike, it's redoing, and of course, redoing, day after day, is what a hotel is all about. Different guests, same incessant demands: my pillow is too hard, too soft, the tea is too weak, too strong, too hot, too cold, there is sand on the floor, in my bed, on the beach.

If guests, like fish, stink after three days, I had a hulking heap of them and it was all I could do not to put a clothespin on my nose. Except that I could have worn a tin pot on my head and not a single guest would have noticed. I, like any servant, was a non-entity, invisible. Except, of course, when there was sand on the floor.

As for Gil, he would not pretend to care that the surf was too noisy or the moon too bright for these guests, immune to satisfaction. He left it to me, and whether I cared seemed beneath his notice.

The Chatham Beach Hotel had gone up quickly, and just as quickly, it filled with guests. I had written the copy for advertisements in the Boston and Providence newspapers. A brochure describing the inn's attractions included photographs. The borders were printed in dark green, Gil's favorite color. Instead of the Lodge coat of arms, I designed a new one, a crest with four swans and a shield of blue and white, for our little ones who had flown away.

The advertisements and brochures were probably a waste of money, for the class of people who find it amusing to bag a hundred birds in a day are a close-knit group. It wasn't only the sports but also their wives who talked up the hotel and kept it fully booked. Sea bathing was popular, and ours was the only hotel on the beach. The young society men for whom Gil had once worked as a guide were now of an age and girth to want the ease of walking a short distance for an afternoon's shooting, after which they could retire to the gunroom for libations before joining the ladies at table. And of course, the chance to dine at Captain Lodge's table was an added draw.

I had wondered if a meal would ever be served there, such was the difficulty of getting the cast-iron cookstove down the beach. It was too unwieldy to bring by boat, and too heavy to be driven across the ford. Gil had loaded it on a wagon and driven it to the crossing when the tide was just finishing its ebb. They laid down a double row of barrels with boards on top. The horses pulling, the men pushing, they half floated, half rolled the stove across the ford. It took six men to lift it back up into the wagon for the two-mile ride down the beach. Even so, the team could hardly go ten steps before Gil would have to stop, get out, and lay down planks for the cart to roll up and out of the sandy ruts.

My work consisted of confirming reservations, being congenial to the guests, and arranging for the ladies' entertainment when the men were hunting. Gil could always escape to the life-saving station, but I had no such relief. There were days when I imagined putting a bit of soapy water in the chowder, just enough to make the guests quick-step to the facilities. My hope would have been to shorten their stay, but not necessarily prevent their coming back. I suppose the entire experience was so overwhelming that even in my dislike I was ambivalent.

SEVENTY-ONE

MY DUTIES AT THE HOTEL WERE SO CONFINING, I could no longer make the crossing and go to the house down by the saltworks to keep watch over Fiji. My whalebone shuttle became my solace. Fortunately, tatting was a socially acceptable thing to do while sitting with the ladies who found it too hot, too windy, too whatever to venture outside onto the piazza overlooking the sea. I reminded them of the excellent sea bathing, but they didn't seem to think it worth the trouble to put on their bathing costumes if there were no men around to admire them. And who would want to swim with one of those ridiculous outfits weighing you down. It made me think of all the times Gil and I had swum naked together, the water slipping over us, hands flowing like currents, seeking eddies and caves.

The weekly life-saving drill was the only thing that could pry these ladies from the parlor, until Gil finally put a stop to it. But not until he had allowed Letitia Barnes, whose husband was president of a Boston bank, to insert herself into one of the drills. It was a sure sign that Gil's mind was neither on the hotel nor the station.

Mrs. Barnes had already picked the story out of Gil concerning the latest rescue. The next day, when Mackey was all set in the breeches buoy and Cahoon was ready to haul him down the line, she insisted on playing the poor, shivering, terrified victim of the nasty, awful storm.

— You are altogether too blasé about this, sir, she said to Mackey, all the while looking at Gil. You don't look a thing like a shipwrecked person should look. Let me show you how.

Mackey cut his eyes over to Gil, who shrugged.

Cahoon loosened the line, dropping Mackey to the ground. Mackey clambered out and gingerly offered to help her, not sure where or what to grasp. But Mrs. Barnes, looking at Gil to make sure he was watching, hiked her dress to step into the oiled canvas breeches suspended from the life-ring, the frilled layers of her pantaloons dangling. Her crinoline rucked up from under her skirts so that she looked like an aging ballerina wearing canvas pants under her tutu. The men cranked down from the drill mast, the line tightened, and she began her downward slide, toward the dune that represented dry land.

She shrieked and flailed, until Gil remarked, loud enough for everyone to hear: With that mouth hanging open, she would have drowned for sure by now, would have swallowed enough rainwater, never mind seawater, like a fool chicken drowning itself in five minutes flat during a spring shower.

When Cahoon had secured the breeches buoy and stood looking anywhere but at her, she pretended to faint, only coming around when she heard Gil's voice, saying, Ride's over. Get out of there before I dunk you in the ocean.

If Gil had a theory, it was that by letting a woman make a fool of herself he would be rid of her; that was disproved. Neither was he correct that being extraordinarily rude would accomplish the same. More women showed up, eager to "take a ride in those britches of yours, Captain Lodge," so that he quietly changed the hour of the drill to early morning, when the ladies would still be sleeping. When they arrived at the station, asking about the start of the drill, Gil ignored them. Mackey, polite, told the women that, thanks to all their encouragement, the crew had perfected the drill and were ready for the season.

Meanwhile, I was stuck with them, the ladies. Somehow I managed to seem engaged, asking questions even as my thoughts ran elsewhere.

Truly, your boy can play Chopin's *Étude, Opus 25, Number 11*, and he not yet fourteen? I find the hedonism in Wilde's *Picture of Dorian Gray* fascinating, have you read it? Your couturier is saying combinations of yellow and purple, emerald and pink will be popular, but what of the new, fuller sleeves, will you wear them?

As the women chattered on, I tatted as though the universe depended on it, as if without my chain of knots, the world would fall apart.

These guests were too self-absorbed to ask to see my work, and it was a good thing, for I could not have explained it, at least not to them. They were accustomed to lace-edged handkerchiefs, antimacassars, lifeless things suitable only for sneezing into or spreading across the back of a chair. Even my fish and birds might have made more sense to these women than this, my most recent work. For in my mind, I was tatting the universe, or more precisely, the empty spaces within it.

So imagine a cobweb, more air than spun silk. What if, like a spider, I could tat the sky? How to define such blue vacancy, except to stitch, bird by bird, cloud by cloud, moth by moth, a vaporous web keeping the firmament held on high. What, then, of the empty, contemptuous sea? Held together by the tenuous crisscrossing of fish swimming their invisible paths, perhaps the oceans would drain away to nothing without these fins to stroke the Pacific, the Indian, the Atlantic alive. The black gaping holes between stars? The Greeks spun entire worlds out of these blank spaces, conjuring gods who loved and fought and envied and died, tracing the arcs of their triumph and strife across the night sky. And so why not I?

When the women rise to prepare their toilettes in anticipation of their husbands' return from the day's shooting, I am free to walk down on the beach and out of sight.

Standing in the rush of waves, I feel the blood start between my legs. Then the moon swells as another month passes, and it begins again, the lunar flow, as I lie abed, sheets speckled red. Month after month, constellations wheel unceasingly overhead, Leo to Virgo to Libra. At the store in town, I walk the narrow boards, reaching up for a hank of yellow thread from the shelf, and feel the familiar enemy trickle. By the time I can walk home, the blood has traced rivers down my legs to pool in my shoes. My footprints are red on the bedroom floor. Beach to bed to bath, bloody knots that spool out, weaving a useless blanket, no baby to comfort.

SEVENTY-TWO

BEFORE THE FIRST SEASON WAS ENDED, it was apparent the hotel was a success. Gil began to enlarge it a second time the very next winter, just as I, at long last, enlarged our family.

When I brought this boy home, I was sure it would make Gil happy. A living, breathing boy, with white-blond hair and eyes the color of honey. My sister's boy, and so, bearing the stamp of me once removed.

This boy gainfully mine, unlike the others. Who could fault me for laying claim to an orphan?

Now we have Ezra, who seems to be settling in nicely even though he keeps insisting we call him by the name my sister gave him, Zeke, Ezekiel Lawrence. Gil doesn't call him by either, as if by naming him out loud, Gil will become responsible for him. But I think Ezra Lodge is a fine name, one he will grow into with time.

An act of charity, it was said, taking in young Ezra, whose father had the bad luck to die at sea and was sewn into the very sail he had grommeted, rigged, hauled, mended, and furled. In his canvas coffin, he'd been laid out feet first on a plank, graced with a few words, and then tilted over the side like a sack of rotting potatoes. The flying jib that had once made invisible currents of air manifest in the shape of billow and luff, now at last too patched to catch and hold the wind, turned and spun on currents of water, not air. No resting place or foothold for petrels in the furled sheet as it tumbled down, the seams his own hands had sewn worried apart by the tender lips of fish, anxious to feed amid the canvassy folds like any contour of rock or coral or seaweed, until his flesh, consumed, would take on the arch of fin or flat fish's orb or crab's barbed claw, his picked-over bones left to spiral downward amid the threadbare remnants of sail. No grave for this Ezra to visit or to pray over, unless he were content to bow his head before the crosscurrent of waves everlasting.

Ezra's father died not knowing a daughter had grown quick in his wife's womb—the seed of both mother and daughter's deaths—not knowing he was leaving his namesake an orphan.

Ezra was to be my redemption. Now that this twelve-year-old boy was here to feed, to clothe, to tuck in at night, this could be enough for me, I thought, and for Gil. A boy to follow him about, to learn the wingbeat of a brant; how to spot a lap of cod, the oily slick blackening the inshore current; how deep to dig for fresh water on a sandbar; all these things would suffice. If we were a family, it would end, me forever unburying, him forever reconsecrating. The rugosas, undisturbed, would bloom again.

Gil, of all people, I thought, would understand my wanting to rethread the lives of our two little ones. For with his birds, hadn't he himself transmuted a poor heap of feathers into a thing seemingly alive, as alive as any being revealed between the moist blink of an eye, that eye a world, that instant filled with belief, better than any interminable death? I look away, and then back, and for me it is enough.

If I could weave the essence of love, this is what the pattern would be. A magical net containing us both, his lips, my eyes, his walk, the tilt of my head.

Our twins had escaped, and so, too, the shipwrecked babe and the whaler's boy. So why not keep this Ezra, such a fine catch, alike as my sister and me, with all the time in the world for Gil to make his mark on the boy.

Didn't I hear Gil singing to that hardy child who survived the wreck, see him bite his little finger like a fish nibbles at bait? So why would he begrudge me that boy's baby brother, washed ashore on the beach like a bolt of cloth, and if the sea stole him in the end, why could he not still be mine, for it was Neptune who first netted him, and not I. I would simply reclaim his lovely symmetry, laying chains of white lace down over the blue of his skin like thready white spume laying its pattern down on blue wave.

Our own two boys and the blue babe, then, who will not cease their crying for want of light and air, but Gil will see them laid back in that darkest of cribs, and my Fiji taken away, too, torn from my arms not an hour after I had made our bed.

They were like stepping stones, these children. The shipwrecked baby, just the age my boys would have been. Then the passage of years, all the children growing, and so why not mine, they should have grown tall as Fiji, my darling four-year-old.

And now here is Ezra, whose head comes just below my chin, exactly where my twins should be, such a sturdy boy that no web could hold him. Ezra, a living, breathing boy who walks upright. The wind in his ribcage blows hot and cold all on its own so I need not tug at him like a puppet on strings.

SEVENTY-THREE

EZRA FOLLOWS GIL AND HIS HUNTING PARTIES, and is already a help to the guests. When the ford is passable at low tide, he rides in the wagon to meet them, the wagon wheels milling water as they cross over from town. If the tide is high, he helps the men into the boat, hauls their excitable retrievers out of the water, and settles the dogs between the thwarts.

I have taught Ezra the names, common and Latin, of our shorebirds, and how to recognize them by their call and coloration. The sandpipers in all their variety, alike as grains of sand reticulated in their small ways: the red-breasted sandpiper (*Trinya canutus*), the purple sandpiper (*Trinya maritima*), the pectoral (*Trinya macolata*), the white-rumped (*Trinya fuseicollin*), and the least sandpiper (*Trinya minutilla*), our favorite, that the hunters call peeps or bumblebees.

I've tried to teach him other things, the story of Moby-Dick, the names of knots and how to tie them. But it is Gil, only Gil, who interests him. He observes his every move, asking questions. Gil gives him a job, but seldom gives praise. At the life-saving station, Gil is accustomed to working as a member of a team, but as a hunting guide, he's used to only one assistant—Dash—and Dash doesn't talk back. He's not used to having help with the million tasks a hunting guide must undertake. At least that's what I thought. How could I know he was already timing his departure from Cape Cod, that while I might be calculating how soon to take a cobbler from the oven, he was counting the minutes between tides, imagining that final crossing from beach to town, from town to rail station, from rail station to portside, down the coast til he could once again set foot on Cape Hatteras?

When finally Gil lets Ezra oil the guns, so that both gun and boy smell of whale, the boy is elated. Until he spills the sperm oil, and the privilege is taken away.

— You've done the same thing yourself, I tell Gil. Right on my oriental rug, not to mention Dash's tail. He's just a boy. Don't be so hard on him.

— I'll oil the guns. It's quicker to do it myself, he says. I don't need any help.

Still, Ezra keeps busy. Not yet four a.m., before Gil is even out of bed, I hear Ezra in the next room, his bare feet making a thump on the floor, Dash whining at our door to go to him.

While Gil walks north to the station, Ezra heads south, stopping at each of the twelve boxes sunk in the sand flats. The sinkboxes are placed some six hundred yards apart, the last box nearly at the end of the bar. He bails out each box and sprinkles the floor with white sand. Tireless, he scavenges the beach, gathering armloads of seaweed, and stuffs handfuls here and there to replenish the camouflage. One sportsman commented that he wouldn't follow Ezra over those flats for a single day, "not for the newest hundred-dollar note that was ever printed."

It's still dark when Ezra races the nearly four miles back to the hotel, Dash veering off to chase a wave, trying to entice the boy to play. But he has his mind on his task, and runs up onto the piazza where Gil is talking over the coming day's shooting with the men. Two are waiting for Ezra, slouched in their hammocks, still half asleep. He politely clears his throat a few times, and when that doesn't rouse the men he snaps his fingers at their Labradors, who are sure to get their masters' attention, along with any blame for waking them. Once the hunters are on their feet, Ezra offers to carry their gear and they accept, and then it's back down the beach, all the way to the last box, within sight of Monomoy once the sun rises. A little more water has seeped in. He bails it out and sprinkles more sand.

Just as the sun comes out of the ocean at Nauset Beach, known as the first stop of the east wind, the hunters are in place with their meerschaum pipes and their flasks of water and their loaded guns. Ezra lies on a pile of seaweed back of the blind, oblivious to the stink and the scrape of kelp. The men, seated on the narrow shelf, their heads just in line with the seaweed, have had their morning smoke and are awake now, watching for flocks of peeps or beetleheads, while the decoys on their sticks sit impaled in the sand, waiting for the rising tide to bubble up around them.

Ignoring the men's complaints about the wrack's fishy odor, he whispers instructions, a testament to his adoration for Gil:

— Sir, you're spot on, Cap'n Lodge says don't move the gun barrel from side to side else the birds'll see the glint of the metal...

— You're not like some men, sir, who aggravate Cap'n Lodge, even if he doesn't say. You don't jump up like a jack-in-the box, you let the sea do its work for you, waiting for a wave to run them closer up the strand...

— Cap'n Lodge's taught me, sir, how it's best to err being too much ahead than behind...

— I learned from Cap'n Lodge that after your first shot, the birds will toss, but they're loathe to leave their dead and dying. Sit tight and they'll return...

Ezra whistles them down with a single mellow *Weet*.

Both he and Dash play retriever, collecting the birds scattered limp or flapping weakly, until the tide sluices ankle-deep into the box, and the men have had enough. He carries their seventeen birds, a good day's shooting, back to the hotel as proudly as if he had shot them all himself.

All this Ezra tells me at bedtime, when I've offered to read him a story. But his head is too full of his own day, and all he wants to hear is what Gil has said or thought or wondered. I tell him, one fiction as good as another.

One guest says that Ezra, without the hotel, would be inducement enough to hunt the Chatham Beach flats, but without Ezra, the hotel would lose all attraction. Another says a bird must be deaf to pass by without at least swerving into closer range at Ezra's call.

It may be that the hunters are being kind to an orphan boy, or it may be that they notice Gil's indifference and are simply filling an awkward silence. The day the hunters troop miles down the beach to the sink boxes, only to find Ezra has forgotten to put the shotgun shells in their game bags, or the day he forgets a hunter's birds, leaving them to wash away on the ebbing tide, then the indifference turns to aggravation.

— That's it. I don't have time for this, Gil says. Tell Blythe to give you some chores. Let her clean up after your mistakes.

— Well, you forgot one whole gun, Ezra says. We had a party of six yesterday, not five. I'm not the only forgetful one around here.

— You'd do best not to talk back, I say. He has a lot on his mind. Go sit on the southwest porch out of Gil's line of sight. He'll get over it soon enough.

SEVENTY-FOUR

After just a single day has passed and a new group of hunters has checked in, Gil seems to have lost his preoccupation along with his short temper, and Ezra is back at his side. I tell Gil thank you, but he only shrugs, and I wonder how long his patience will last. He's mentioned, again, the superior hunting at Hatteras, how there's a thousand birds for every one man, how our cape is so overhunted you practically need to draw straws for a decent shot. I don't say that perhaps he's contributed to the waterfowl and shorebirds' demise, hunters invading the beach, staying right on the hunting grounds thanks to his new hotel, how his reputation, not to mention his fancy brochures, have brought them here. And I don't say maybe you're off hunting something else down south, for I can't believe even he could have foreseen that, never mind my own suspicions. Men are always the last to know.

Before long, Ezra has learned, by watching Gil instruct the cook, how to roast shorebirds. He could hardly wait until the next sports staying at the hotel had their chance at a wisp of snipe.

It's lucky the men bagged the birds early in the day, for it's taken him nearly all afternoon to skin their heads and necks and to pluck the reddish-brown feathers and the gray, barred with black. He trusses each snipe, bringing the beak under the wing so that the birds all in a row look like unfeathered young asleep with their heads tucked in, except that their pinions are held fast to their thighs, their legs twisted at the knuckles, and instead of a nest of salt hay they sit upon a thick piece of bread to catch their juices. Finally, he bastes them with butter, Cook helping him dredge them in flour only because it's getting late and the birds need roasting.

When Cook brings the roasted snipe into the dining room and lifts the silver dome from the tray, Ezra is looking not at the birds but at Gil. It hurts to see the shine go out of the boy's eyes when Gil sits silent, looking not at his plate but into his glass, as if some strange sea creature were swimming laps in the claret. As the men compliment the fledgling chef and go on to recite Ezra's hunting tips from earlier in the day, Gil still says nothing. He does not take seconds.

SEVENTY-FIVE

SOMETHING WAKES ME LATER THAT NIGHT. I go to Ezra's room, where the moon is missing from the window, offstage. Enough light to see that Ezra, too, is absent, the bedcovers flung aside, nightshirt in a heap on the floor.

My mind tracking backward, to the silence of disinterest or was it disdain, the bird gone mealy in the boy's mouth, not just dinner spoiled, but back, back to trussing the tucked wings, dredging the featherless bird in flour, further back as the limp body jostled in the game bag, rode in Dash's mouth, back and back to the reflex of finger on steel trigger, intricate flight, back up to the phalanx of wheeling birds, all the way back to fragile shell, horned beak hacking toward freedom, all crashing down with the clink of a single indifferent fork and the dismissive scrape of a chair.

Without waking Gil, I throw his hunting jacket over my night-dress, my mind tracking forward, where would Ezra have gone? I picture him passing what count for landmarks on a changeable beach, whatever might last a tide or two—the half-buried keel of the *Sonnet*, the charred driftwood from a signal fire, a heap of stove-in barrels of rum left by the wreckers.

Running along the surf's edge, following my moon shadow to-ward Gil's Folly, I hear him first, hear the report of a shotgun, and the shattering of glass. By the time I reach the shanty, he has shot out the glass windows Gil had set in the sockets of a whale's eyes, and holding the gun by the barrel, he is bashing Gil's most prized possession, his bespoke Purdey, against the walls, raking off bird wings and fish fins, leaving splintered bones in his wake. When the gunstock hits a whalebone rib, the breech springs open, and he throws down the gun and grabs an oyster rake. Raising it above his head, he drags it down the side of the shanty, feathered shingles peeling away from the wall.

I take the rake from his hands, hold him to my breast, his blond hair dark with sweat, smelling like boy, the pungency of salt and earth.

— It's just his way, I say. Come home. In the morning we'll nail everything back in place so he'll never know you were here.

— I hope he does know! I want him to! I hate him! he shouts.

He breaks free and runs down into the surf. I wait til the sea takes away some of the sting, then put Gil's hunting jacket around his shoulders. Together we walk back to the hotel.

Ezra got his wish. When we went back early the next morning to repair the damage, Gil had already been to the folly, everything tacked back into place as though Ezra had never been there. As if anger could be assuaged with a simple hammer and nails.

As for the scarred bird's eye maple of his Purdey side-by-side, perhaps the stock could be sanded and revarnished, but nothing, it would seem, could smooth out the hard feelings Gil had. For me? For the boy? Blame is a useless salve. Still, I reach for it, applying it liberally to myself.

SEVENTY-SIX

IT WAS I, NOT GIL, who sent the boy away. A technicality, for although I was the one who sat Ezra down and explained that we could no longer keep him, I who packed his bags, who checked the tide, timing the crossing, and drove him to the station, it was Gil who said if the boy doesn't go, I will.

— I can't bear to part with him.

— Then your decision is made.

Of course I sent him away. He went back to Maine, with enough money to ease my guilt, remorse, embarrassment, brokenheartedness, pride.

Perhaps pride was the worst. I was so proud that I had finally given Gil a son. My sister's son, yes, but so aflame with Gil's own passions that Ezra was surely the one boy who could thaw the old sorrow thick as pond ice.

— But he's trying. He tries so hard to please you.

— Blythe, it's you who's trying too hard. You have to stop. Yes, I wanted sons. Sons of my own. But it's over and done.

Ezra could use the money for school when he got older, or to set himself up as a guide. But after he left, I found the cash wadded in the sugar dish, scattered on the table, in the chair seat, on the floor, like so much confetti, celebrating nothing.

I never heard from him again. And not even a tear could I shed for him. It was as though he were a boy I'd dreamed, and like a dream, his appearance and disappearance, in and out of our lives so quickly, a flickering apparition, the very idea of him became vague and faintly unsatisfactory.

Gil went south in the fall. For the excellent hunting, the newspaper said. Yes, I replied to anyone who asked, that's right. Gil says the hunting's unmatched, just like it used to be here.

SEVENTY-SEVEN

HOW TO KNOW YOU CAN LOVE SOMETHING TO DEATH? For the things Gil prized above all, the hunting, the fishing, the foraging, soon felt the effects of his wish to share that wealth with others. Even before the hotel began drawing crowds, Gil had spoken of his concerns. At a special meeting at Town Hall he advocated that something be done about certain persons hunting on the flats and beaches of Chatham. Gil, usually so reserved, gave a "full and studied statement," according to the *Monitor*, favoring the protection of shorebirds and waterfowl, even to the detriment of ladies' bonnets. I have the clipping somewhere, a drawer in his gun cabinet, I believe.

Later he railed against overhunting on the Great West Flat south of the hotel and was livid when an article in *Ornithologist and Oölogist* claimed it wouldn't be long before hunters, in order to be granted passage to the flats, would be required to wear a ticket in their hatbands declaring that ginger pop and cigarettes were bought at our hotel.

At that time, Gil was the only person in Massachusetts not affiliated with a college or university to be granted the authority to take birds out of season for scientific study. He had begun contributing articles to birding journals, including one about the demise of red phalaropes when confronted with certain manmade encroachments.

That was a good time for us, before the hotel was built, before the wreck of the *Phoenician*, before Gil became keeper—those simpler days back when he was just a surfman, when he and I spent long hours at the shanty and all along the beaches. We would tramp the marsh together, and I would make field notes as he dictated: first brant of the season, last turtle hatchlings, first black-bellied plover nest, last fish hawk to set off for South America. Call, coloration, the size and shape of eggs, we dreamed bird dreams, we swam fish. We turned whale flips in tandem, we breathed both air and sea.

Adrift on the water, we spied on birds from our boat. Stretched out lengthwise, we were eye level with jumping mullet, so close they would spatter our faces with spray. We counted their jumps, always hoping for a record-breaking eight, but a fingerling mullet's title of seven skips seemed secure for all time. Circus act or escape artist? We argued over what caused the mullets' agile leaps. I tickled Gil, claiming they jumped for joy. He leaned across, nuzzling my hair, then bit my earlobe. When I jumped, he laughed. Argument over, he said.

Easy in our skins, we were content to watch and wait for what passed before our eyes, the entire world before us, not even needing to turn our heads. Drowsing in the boat, we floated in the strong noonday sun, aimless as any leaf. We watched a school of minnows congregate in the shade of an oar. Finning the still water, they took on the contour of blade, loom, and handle. As if the demarcation between sun and shade were a solid wall, high as the water was deep, the minnows oared hard to remain in place, hiding from the sun. When we looked up, eyes meeting, it was as though Gil and I, too, we were all of one shape, made one with our witnessing.

— You want to know how the world appears to any whale or minnow? I asked. Here, let their seeing flow from your eyes, I said, turning his head in profile, throwing his shadow down on the water. I drew the oar in, and the minnows scattered, then shoaled. Dozens of silver fish the size of my little finger faced into the current. They huddled in the shadow of his familiar profile, taking on the shape of his unrepentant hair, his brow, his nose, his chin.

—What sights, then, are streaming manifold from your schooled and eager eyes? I asked. They are tasting of your tongue, they are breathing saltwater breath through your nostrils, they swim hard against the strong current of your thoughts.

He shook his head and the fish flew outward like water droplets flung.

When the wind was right, we would wade or row to sand flats or intertidal shoals smaller than most houses, eviction notice, the next high tide. With an oyster shell, we outlined rooms in the sand, an open-air shanty for a day, the sky our only roof, and we lay on our outlined bed, a south breeze our blanket. We walked across the wide sweep of the flats, our footprints comprising neither toes nor heels, but craters that made a pool for sand fleas as the tide rushed in.

Our laughter rang down the shore, echoing off the brittle, calcified moon rising up out of the sea, chipped and worn as any ocean-tumbled shell. I would sometimes look back to see if there were two more sets of prints running alongside, four small gashes.

Back at the shanty, we felt closed in after spending all day in our open-air unceilinged house. The room was now crowded with a velvet armchair he'd hauled over to the beach for me. After the first hard blow, the chair wore a crisp white glaze of salt that had first clung to my form so that a shadow of me always sat there. More often, we both sat on the floor, boots upended by the door, just as on that first day when I arrived, no calling card in hand. Using one of the chair's eelgrass cushions for a backrest, Gil would sit with his long legs outstretched, leaving me only enough room to put my head in his lap, my own legs running up the wall so that the soles of my feet seemed a roost for his birds sitting on the shelf above, my skirts in a heap at my waist like a silken nest. I could wait, barely, for him to seek out the small patch of blond curled in the center of the nest.

But first, by the light of the fire, he would dictate some bit of bird talk for submission to an ornithology journal. My quill pen would wait on his words. When he finally began to speak it was as though my nib were flowing not with India ink, but with watercolor paints, so vivid were his descriptions. Together we painted a turnstone word by word across the page, coloring the bird in patches of light red and chestnut, irregularly splashed with black and white and dark brown, tail white with dusky patches near the tips, wing coverts mottled with chestnut and black, eyes and bill black, feet pale orange.

It didn't matter to him that these turnstones, these "chicken plovers," are common as barnyard hens. The first to describe their aerobatics and their able seamanship, he'd been lauded by those who care about such things. And if a turnstone is common as any chicken, his recent sighting of avocets, exceptionally rare visitors here, had caused great excitement amongst his fellow ornithologists.

Now, reversing positions, his head on my lap, my tablet propped on my knees, I take down his words, describing the rare *Recurvirostra americana* making a noisy landing, swimming strongly, coming ashore to wade in salt pools deep enough to immerse their entire heads and necks, feathered a deep cinnamon brown, their striking white plumage glistening with droplets of water. Together we describe their black interscapulars, the short, squarely cut tail a soft pearl gray, the black bill, long and slender, upcurved. The words flow a dull, pale blue, coloring its stilted legs. Its iris bright red, my quill drops to the floor, no time now for words, the birds at last fly away. A single line of ink trails errant down the page, an alphabet all its own, now faint from years of my lone finger's translation. Over and over, the line speaks, whenever I ask it, saying *Ahh, yes. Please. More.*

However vivid this indulgence, it fails to supplant that other memory, my one brief look at *her*, brevity no measure of how long a memory lingers.

SEVENTY-EIGHT

No easy way to get from Cape Cod to Cape Hatteras in the winter of 1893, and who, other than reprobates and drifters, would want to? I carried only a small carpetbag with a nightgown and a comb and one change of clothes, for I didn't intend to stay long. Chatham to Boston, a succession of trains. New York, then Philadelphia, Baltimore, and Richmond, on down to Norfolk and over to Elizabeth City, where I boarded the *Hattie Creef* for Roanoke Island, last stop before catching the mailboat to Hatteras.

Over four days' travel, there'd been time enough to read and reread the letter Gil had left in plain sight on his desk at the life-saving station, time to write and rewrite my reply never sent. This was a message that could only be delivered in person, like a right hook, or a kiss. I'd come to fetch my husband home.

After disembarking in Manteo, I spent the night at the Tranquil House. The mailboat wouldn't leave for several hours, so I ventured into Griffin & Sample's, well-stocked with all manner of fishing gear, and pictured Gil buying a hand line or sinkers. As for the milliner's, I didn't bother. The hat styles displayed in the window were at least two years and more behind, if I cared about such things, which I didn't, and still don't. That comb, thrown in my bag as an afterthought, represented the extent of my vanity, which needs tending only every few days or so. Gil always loved how the wind would dress my hair, just before his fingers would reach nape or temple, rearranging the pale strands to his liking.

A woman, none too friendly, directed me to the far end of the wharf for the final leg of my journey. The fumes from the naphtha gas engine were even more noxious than the *Hattie Creef's*, so I wasn't feeling my best when hours later I arrived at the north end of Hatteras Island, called Chicamacomico. Even now I feel the syllables rattle like shotgun pellets against the roof of my mouth. The postal officials in Washington deemed the jumble of vowels and consonants unpronounceable, and so the government renamed it Rodanthe, which to my mind wasn't much better. From the Algonquin, Chicamacomico: "Swept Place." Or "Land of Sinking Sands." The Indians' place names aptly described it.

When I stepped onto the landing, it seemed the biggest waste of a federal dollar I'd ever seen, to think such an outpost was even deserving of mail delivery, like selling stamps and sorting mail in the Sahara, just as barren and just as sparsely populated. A gap-toothed man leaned against a sloop, its starboard planks staved in. He roused up, flicked the stub end of a cheroot into the marsh, and looked me over, nodding to himself. I might have wondered, did someone telegraph my arrival, except that in my experience, islanders' gossip has little need for dots and dashes. Then again, it took some of both, a whisper here, a telegram there, for the Freemasons and the Life-Saving Service to alert me to the news they'd found Gil living here under a different name.

— Which way, sir, to the— but without a word, he pointed down the beach to a house standing slightly askew. The only other building in sight was the life-saving station, its starkly beautiful watchtower piercing the sky.

I made my way across the sand, skirts dragging, a thick ground fog giving the illusion of treading water, on past the station, without seeing a soul. The house appeared well-kept except that, sandpapered by the wind, most of its white paint was gone, leaving it a stippled gray. I climbed the three porch steps flanked by piles of driftwood, the tips of the branches sprouting conch shells like white blossoms tinged with pink. These people, it seemed, made do with what they had, whatever or whoever washed ashore.

I would have knocked if I'd cared about manners. I don't, especially since it had taken five months to find him. In the front door, through the dim hallway of the shotgun house, and then out the back, the porch door slamming behind me. Gil, lounging on the top step, glanced up, and given the look of surprise on his face, I can promise you neither islanders' gossip nor telegrams had reached him. And on hers: this girl leaning against the porch post, a half-naked goose stretched across her lap. Gray feathers floated between them, catching first in his stiff shock of black hair, then drifting to her waist-length hair blacker still in its glossiness, swept back from her face by a widow's peak.

Gil recovered, or else he feigned it with a half-smile, those blue eyes looking up at me through salt-tipped lashes.

— Caught, he said.

— Depends who's fishing, I replied.

The girl looked from me to Gil and then back. — You're—?

— I am.

With the bird's long neck dangling over the crook of her arm, she swept the loose feathers away, pulled the goose's skin taut, and continued her plucking, but not before she stole another look at my husband. Call her a child if you will. But she knew what she was about, even at the age of twelve.

Gil stood and walked to the end of the wraparound porch, his back to both of us, and stared out at the breakers appearing and then disappearing as the fog began to drift in tatters across the endless sweep of beach.

— All right, Blythe, he said. Let's go home.

SEVENTY-NINE

If you could map lovemaking like an astronomer maps the sky, or an oceanographer charts the bottom of the sea, how would ecstasy's terrain appear? Would it be a range of mountain peaks and valleys, a geographical tour of tongue's tip tracing hollowed throat? A finger's width, the road circling ankle or inner wrist? Or would a cartographer trace the ridgeline where hip meets hip, and on down the escarpment of legs entwined?

Of course, each seismic, continent-shifting quake would be charted, crevices revealed. But what of the passing glance that circles back and holds? The breathless, breathy kiss passed back and forth between parted lips, the whispered name, the wrenched cry held between white teeth? How to chart the blush that, insistent as any spring tide, rises from the depths in a slow sweep?

Perhaps the map should extend beyond our own archipelago to encompass the twisted sheet, the heeled furrows in the sand, the net seized in a one-fisted grasp. A contour map, what lies below, the trail of matted hay through the salt meadow, ending in a starred swirl of straw that will take three seasons to regrow our shapes. Or what lies above, the wings of the swan slanting over our heads, until the night he comes crashing down, jolted loose from the bedframe, his feathers tickling a fit of laughter, all muffled in a white nested clutch.

There are endless ways to love, and to be loved, and I tatted them all.

Opposite my bed, once-white lace hangs against blue wall. My eyes no longer wander its beggared countryside. After all this time, I have no need for tramping vagrant territory, no chance of ever again becoming lost in its socketed caves, its knobbed cliffs, still familiar as my own body, or his.

The upper third of the tapestry is richly patterned, so that only specks of blue shine through, the threads laid and overlaid like fingers interlaced. Further down the wall, as love's grip loosens, the weave begins to unravel, so that all along the bottom, thin strands reach out, seeking a connection no longer there.

Yellowed with age, any threadbare gaps restrung by spider silk, it's a map where there is no *X* to mark what was pirated from me all those years ago by a twelve-year-old named Maud, she who, in the space of a few short years, would become the second Mrs. Lodge.

On the night I finished knotting the last tasseled fringe, Gil had just come in from a swim, droplets of water running down his back. A day-old growth of beard etched his jawline, still glowing faintly with the sea's phosphorescence. I trailed my fingers across his cheek and held them to the light. The ridges and furrows of my fingertips glittered as if set with diamonds before the light died back down to bare flesh.

I wondered if the ocean's fleeting jewels turned his mind back to that August night when I arose naked out of the sea to hand him a clam shell; the sea, the shell, my body streaming light, while overhead the Perseids hurled stars down from the sky. I wondered if he remembered how the dark water flickered and smoldered, lit from above and below, as if heaven and hell were vying for each wave's crushed or crashing soul.

He turned away. The answer, then, both yes and no.

I laid out the map on the bed, its nether reaches blank as the unknown new world of a loveless life, territory so foreign it could have been another planet. I showed him its landmarks, our deepest gaze and most tender caress, each bone-clenching precipice and pooled waterfall. He stood looking, not blinking, stood still. I lay down and wrapped myself in its dwindling embrace.

He curled himself around me, but did not stay. The woven strands must have been a barrier thick as any brick wall, for he gently unfurled me and gathered the lace in his hands. He draped it across his squared shoulders, browned skin revealed through the gapped knots, and without looking back, turned and went out the door.

It was one of many leave-takings over the next five years, as though by tatting the map of our love, I had handed him his own atlas of escape.

And what of his homecomings? He would walk in the door unabashed after days or weeks or months. Like some ticket or token, over the back of a chair he would lay the map, or on the table place the clam shell, or under my chin stroke the feather that had coaxed uncounted flights. It was never the lace or the shell or the feather, tokens of shared memories; it was the one-sided smile, the saunter, the blue eyes that sought, found, and locked. Like some dog-eared ticket stub, those familiar gestures were always worth the price of admission.

Brushing past me, he would walk into the kitchen, hungry, for what? Perhaps something as simple and as complicated as an ordinary day. I would stand straight, chin lifted, and follow, knowing my own starvation was imminent, the only uncertainty when.

I could have woven those, too, his comings and goings, shuttling between two worlds, hers and mine. I could have tatted his silhouette filling the doorframe, his shrugs, his knee braced against the tiller, his shouldered glance. Hello and goodbye each carried its own fill and lack.

There were the times I might not know he had left again. Lulled back into the rhythm of a shared life, I would assume he was off hanging a net or cutting brush for a duck blind. But when the candle had burned down and the bluefish on his plate sat congealed in its own oil, I would go and look, and find the shell gone, or the feather, or the hair clasp.

With just as little warning, one day the door would open and I could hardly bear to look, in case it was the wind.

I don't need an excuse to come back, I told you I'd always be back, he would say, ambling toward me, palms open.

Later, the missing clam shell or the hair clasp would appear. So perhaps not a ticket or a token, these beloved objects were a secret kiss hello, a kiss goodbye, until the day he left for good, when I found them carefully mapped within a circumference of lace, the unmade bed still holding the shape of our sleep. I set them out as idols, worshipped on the altar of a vanished love.

Why weave his comings and goings, the pattern of our lives? From beneath blue eyelids, open or shut, his absence is all I see.

EIGHTY

ILLNESS IS AN UNINTENDED IMPORT. This one stowed away on a clipper from France and quickly made headlines. The Monitor *was filled with* advertisements posing the question, "Suffering from Insanity? Suicides Alarmingly Prevalent! Would You Be Rid of the Awful Effects of La Grippe? There Is But One Sure Remedy That Never Fails, viz. Dana's Sarsaparilla!" There were enough companies making and selling such quackery that soon one had to wonder whether there was something to it—something more than just the delirium that can accompany a high fever.

Gil was the last man at the station to come down with the illness. It was fortunate there were no shipwrecks during that time. Even though stations to the north and south were instructed to be ready to assist, those crews, too, were afflicted.

Of course, even if the respiratory difficulties hadn't been so severe, any one of several so-called cures would have been enough to ground the men. Gil had left only long enough to replenish the station's stores of castor oil and quinine, but that was sufficient time for the crew to have come up with a supposed cure, a milk punch of Jamaica and Santa Cruz rums. It was doubtful whether the main ingredient of this remedy, peptogenic powder, ever made it into the concoction. Between that and a hot grog of coca wine, the men would have been too inebriated, never mind too weak from illness, to have rescued a cat out of a tree, much less been able to launch a surfboat so heavy it takes a draft horse to cart it down the beach. And all the practice in the world wouldn't have been sufficient to aim the Lyle gun at a ship bobbing in and out of sight between rows of breakers.

I suppose I must agree that the men at the station suffered from the febricular rather than the catarrhal form of the illness, with its aggravated feeling of "the blues." Three years earlier, the Paris epidemic of *influenza melancholia* was blamed for a twenty-five percent increase in suicides.

Gil's superior in the Life-Saving Service, in writing of his disappearance in September of 1893, described his air of distractedness, his unreasonable worries about financial matters, and the severity of his case.

He never actually said Gil was insane. Ezra might have had a different opinion, but then, what might be my own excuse?

Where is the dividing line between sanity and insanity? Is it a feverish thing, or does it sit quiet, precarious, in some hidden crevice of the mind, waiting patient and watchful, between utter boredom and the risk of dare?

If life is lived between the lines, what vitality, what passion for movement, restless change, comes out of that timeless, still place between tides? I once watched Gil hang from his waist at the edge of the dock, his face flushed with blood, waiting to see the exact time when the tide turned, watching for, what would it take, how long would it last, one second, two, ten? It may be there's no such thing—the intersection of time and space when there is no ebb, no flow, only slack water, unless there in the slack water something still moves, something potent, portending, containing all possibilities, boding change.

Perhaps sanity is a daily series of small choices: I pick up the knife. I slice my wrist. Or perhaps a pear. Then again, I might bite into the overripe fruit, the juice running down my wrist, and simply flirt with the blade, a frisson of *what if* running down my finger piercing my heart before I open the drawer and toss the knife in amongst the spoons.

I don't know if he ever discovered it, that subtle turn. Perhaps it was something beyond sight, a vibration, perhaps what a fish feels, water displaced along its length, directing its movement in relation to unseen currents, so that an entire school can veer and converge in the instant it takes to angle a thousand fins. Perhaps Gil, too, had this sensibility, something he used to navigate his world, to orient his life, to escape mine.

EIGHTY-ONE

WHY DID MY ENTIRE LIFE HAVE TO BE LAID BARE in a newspaper fit only for wrapping fish guts to be thrown behind the net shed for feral cats to fight over? First, his disappearance. "Some say there's a woman in it." Then speculation—he was in New York, he was in North Carolina, no it was South Carolina, what's the difference, somewhere down South, close enough. Then his discovery. "His wife found him wandering, barefoot and disheveled in the woods." That juicy item made it into *The New York Times*. Then his return, demoted to the Chatham *Monitor*. "He is just not like what he was before." All the to-ing and fro-ing, each fall and spring, the correspondent dutifully reported over the next five years, until finally the marriage announcement, no mention of the requisite divorce. "The man with two families." I don't recall if that phrase made it into print or was just passed by word of mouth.

All the rumors. It was la grippe, it was insanity caused by la grippe, it was the shame, the wreck of the *Phoenician*, it was worries over money even though he had investments in the thousands, she was too old, she was so young, words words words, knowing nods, on and on and on. Too bad I couldn't wrap people's still-wagging tongues in the newspaper along with rank day-old fish.

Every fall, according to the newspaper, "He went south, for the shooting." Poor choice of punctuation, why not an ellipsis instead of a comma, let the hesitation weigh heavily, coy in its millisecond of a pause.

The sad truth of it is, the headline should have read: He went far. She stayed near. They each lived the opposite in their minds. For I believe he never stopped thinking of me, that he lived out his days in his mind, where I live mine, dreaming *us*. The two of us, and all our dear boys.

EIGHTY-TWO

IT'S ANOTHER WARM DAY, yet the house keeps its hold on the chill of the previous night, and so a good day for a fire. I wouldn't bother, but Dash loves to sit and stare at the flames, and sometimes it soothes these stiff joints of mine so that I can take up a piece of tatting. Moving wood from porch to bin to hearth is likely the only reason I still get around as well as I do at my age. I can only carry one log at a time, cradling it in my arms.

With my hands full, I must use my elbows, bracing against tables and the backs of chairs. I'll just pretend I'm wading back into the surf. That swim earlier this week was delightful. And now, the warmth of a fire will be just the thing, if I can find the matches.

I once made a mistake of docking myself against one of the piles of journals stacked high. The magazines came foaming down, the pages overlapping in a white tide that ran all the way to the piano, where they pooled around the ebony leg. Since I no longer play, they aren't in the way, and so I've left them there. It didn't seem important. But now I see it through Gilly's eyes. After I start the fire, I'll sit on the piano bench and see if I can get them in order. Maybe she'd like to leaf through them after she gets back from her walk, a break to clear her head, she said. I can only imagine.

She should be back soon, so it's good to take the chill off, get rid of the seaweedy smell, or maybe it's moldy in here. Those black spots on the journals, I can't make out whether it's mildew or just the smattering of letters on the page.

On the porch, I prop the door open and pick up a small log. Dash retrieves a bundle of kindling. He acts as my rudder, leaning in on me as we tack across the room. Dash is the one who likes her. I'm only doing this to humor him. I wonder what she'll try to pry out of me today.

When Gilly arrives, Dash nearly beats her to death with that tail of his, but I tell her not to let it go to her head.

— It's not you he's excited over. I told him we were going to the beach.

She turns her head and cuts her eyes, so blue between the black lashes. If the careless slamming of a door can be inherited, so, too, I suppose, can a tilt of the head.

— Hmmph. I know it's me you're excited to see. Both of you, she says, grinning.

Please don't let me see those white teeth through parted lips, I think. Not again. The missing becomes too much.

She says she wants to see the shanty. How long does she think a birdwing or a dorsal fin can last in the wind coming in off Chatham Bar? Not as long as it took for me to accept Gil was never coming back, at least not to stay, and which of the two was worse, it's plagued me all my life.

I tell her to get the flask from my coat pocket, fill it with cognac, and be quick about it, before we miss the crossing at high tide and have to walk.

For years, I'd made half-hearted attempts to patch the Folly's increasingly denuded walls, its weather-pocked holes. But it seemed sad, the contrast between old and new: pebbled sharkskin rich as any fine leather an affront to the bleached skin of a stingray's fin; the clean, bright wings of birds an insult to wind-shredded quills. So I let it go, though I still visit what's left of it, or spy on it through the glass on days I'm not up to crossing over to the beach.

The outer trappings of Gil's Folly are long gone, but the whale-bones are still there, leaning in on themselves, unless the wind has colluded with the tides, burying the past altogether.

It feels wonderful to be in the boat, and away. She handles the dory with ease, and before I can even give her our bearings, she reads the shoals, heading straight for the channel.

The beach is wide and clean, and at first I think I must have been mistaken. But she spots the whalebones rising up like rafters, and we make our way to all that remains of Gil's Folly. Leaning against the smooth white bones, we pass the flask back and forth. The brandy burns my throat, a good excuse to let her talk.

— Finish telling me about the sea oats, I say.

She picks up the story, tells how he steered the shadboat toward Bodie Island.

— What was its name, the boat, I ask.

— I held the paint bucket, she says, the day he lettered it down along the bow. I sounded it out. *The Wild Onion.*

At that, I finish the cognac in one large swig. She can think it's the burn of the alcohol that's cause for tears, instead of hearing from her lips, so like his, my nickname, Wild Onion, the name he gave me here beneath these same overarching bones. I smell the coppery blood, the wet feathers, I see the canvas game bag emptied of the afternoon's shooting, a brace of black ducks, I hear Dash, the very first in a long line of Chessies, whining high in his throat, recounting his own version of the hunt. I smell the strings of dried herbs hanging from the rafters, and the fresh-picked thyme, the sliced apples, crisp and tart, and the wild onions with their odor of secret mineral earth lying in a heap on the table. He strips the pungent green shoots from the fringed white bulbs and, thrusting one between my teeth, he dares me not to cry. I feel his tongue on my collarbone as he chases stray tears. With one foot, he pushes Dash out the door.

If she's noticed my reaction, she doesn't show it, but continues on. She tells how, once he'd cranked the motor, the shadboat burst like a cork out of Maggie's Drawers into John's Ditch, and on into Broad Creek. He bought two Orange Crushes at Cap'n Pugh's store in Wanchese, and they stood drinking them, cold and tangy, while talking to Screenwire and Tucker as they tarred a net.

Once back in the boat, *The Wild Onion*, she says again, making me reach for the empty flask, they steer out of the mouth of Broad Creek and into the open waters of Pamlico Sound where there's nothing to break the wind.

— Hoist it, Papa, hoist the sail now! she shouts. Cut the engine so we can hear, so you can ask me the birds. I'll close my eyes, no peeping. The gulls are noisy, they don't count. I hate it when you can't hear the water chocking against the side of the boat. If it's quiet I can tell you kingfisher or osprey. Besides, your old motor is smelly. Turn it off.

But he's in a hurry to reach Bodie Island and steers southeast of the Roanoke Marshes, not stopping at the fish camps hiked up on stilts that from sea level look like gray barnacles latched onto brown marsh.

— What's our bearing? he asks as he trims the tiller.

— East! Well, east southeast, but soon we'll see the club, and then we'll be headed straight into the morning sun.

— Not this time of year. In spring, the sun's zenith is more northerly.

The low buildings of Bodie Island Hunt Club come into sight, their weathered gray inked black, silhouetted by the sun. As they approach the dock, she scuttles to the bow, barefoot like her father on this cool spring morning, her knickers creased one extra turn so the cuffs won't catch her heels. In two strides he joins her, taking the bow line she hands up to him and tossing it loosely around the piling.

— We're cowboys! Let me lasso it!

But he's already begun heaving the burlap sacks onto the pier, the seeds hissing as they resettle. The bags mound higher on the dock, high as Jockey's Ridge, she says.

— Will our dunes grow as high?

— There are only a few places on the Banks where the confluence of wind and shoreline can build the sand into high dunes, he says. Name them.

— North to south?

He nods yes.

— Penny's Hill, Run Hill, Kill Devil Hill, the Seven Sisters, Jockey's Ridge. Then they stop. Why, Papa?

— There's no woods to catch the sand, not until you get to Buxton Woods, and by then, Cape Hatteras is fending off the wind.

— Wash Woods, Kitty Hawk Woods, Nags Head Woods, she chants.

— Not Wash Woods. All that's left there are tree stumps. At Chicamacomico and Kinnakeet, there aren't even stumps to show for the maritime forests that once grew there, although the old-timers recall when a hurricane uncovered them for a day.

— What happened to the trees?

— Cut for ships' timbers. Just like Cape Cod.

There, he said those two words, not me, she thinks, but decides to test the waters.

— Where our seeds came from?

He nods, moving the last of the bags from the boat to the dock, and begins loading the wheelbarrow.

— Where you came from?

He piles four of the burlap bags into the barrow, sets her on top, and heads east, toward the ponds.

The dirt hammers small fists against the mahogany box, each man's shovelful rapping against the wood that will grow into a tree, the rapping now muffled as dirt strikes dirt, not wood, the hole filling slowly as the shovels arc high against the sky. A bluebird day, the hunters call it, when the sky is crisp with cold, a day for duck hunting. Papa would be at Bodie Island, then, on a day like today.

Before she came north to see me, Gilly says, she went to Bodie Island. The dunes she and her father had built caught at her ankles, the sand spilling down into her new shoes, the sky a brighter blue than the dark blue of the Red Cross uniform she wore, against regulations, but who would know?

She could make out two hunters in brush blinds at the edge of the fresh pond, an oval mirror tilted skyward. The dune line she and her father had farmed for a season, planting it first with pine saplings and then sea oats, had grown higher over the years, protecting the true crop, the wild celery and submerged grasses harvested each year by the ducks, geese, and swans, another step in the chain that ended with the men from Boston who came south to hunt.

It was the right decision to sail to Bodie Island rather than walk to the Manteo Cemetery, a few blocks from home, to say her goodbyes to her father. In the cemetery there was no mahogany tree playing tag with its shadow, no eighteen rings of growth spiraling out from his passing. Only a stone bearing his name, two dates, and the places marking his coming and his going. So she'd gone to Bodie Island, hoping to find him in the golden oats flagging the dunes, or the flashing blue eye of the fresh pond, or if not there, in the very chemistry of the air, dense with minerals, the smell of quartz and salt and iodine, of phosphorus and marsh gas and blood, his chemistry, and hers.

She reaches into her pocket and takes out a handful of sea oats.

— Here, she tells me. I was going to toss these to the wind—they belong here. But you know, I think they should be yours to scatter.

EIGHTY-THREE

I'VE DECIDED TO GIVE MY TATTED WEDDING GOWN TO GILLY. But she surprises me, sharing an intimacy, tells me it's too late for that. Which makes me wonder, how long does it take for one's ring finger to become accustomed to the fit of a thin gold band? Or perhaps the better question, how long till the finger forgets?

Never. Like a key designed to fit the tumblers of a single lock, a girl's finger will ache for the ring placed upon it long after it's gone.

Gilly's finger wore her husband's gold band for all of six days, the length of time it took her mother to have the marriage annulled. With that Maud for a mother, I'm surprised it took six days, until Gilly tells me they were able to keep it secret for five.

A tall slouchy boy who went barefoot most of the year, who ate what he could forage or net or draw a bead on, who used sand instead of soap to scrub himself clean, whose bed was dune-shaped or hay-hollowed or hard as a skiff's juniper chine—this young man might be able to survive on that rugged coast, but could he stand up to the likes of Maud Lodge? He could.

I must say I admire anyone who, when told he was unfit to stand in the presence of her daughter, could look upon the likes of Maud Lodge and offer, "Yes, ma'am, never claimed to be. Neither to stand by her nor lay beside her. But I did. And it was fine. I assure you, it was fine," and then wink at the girl as he shoved off from the dock, putting the gold band in his one unripped pocket.

If Jake Scarborough reminded Maud of the kind of man she refused to let Gil be, I suspect she was right. That Gilly let Jake leave was a restless bed of her own making, for whom else does a young girl fall in love with, absent a father, but one just like him.

Gilly misses these two men, but is it them she misses, or does she ache for the empty space she thought they filled? And how will she ever know, unless she herself can fill it?

I'll give her the tatted gown. I think she'll someday find a reason to wear it, if only in remembrance of me.

EIGHTY-FOUR

THE DAYS ARE STARTING TO WIND DOWN. You can feel it in the air, a crisp tang. In the wind's direction, northeasterly. In the subtle change in light, a warm gold, the sun setting due west as the fall equinox approaches. Even without all these signs, it's there, the heaviness in my chest that portends *Away*.

Gilly, all wrapped up like a going-away present, dressed in her Red Cross uniform, has sensed it. Perhaps she's concluded, even at this young age, that a watch on your wrist is simply a piece of jewelry that ticks, that the true measure of time, exquisitely precise, is all around, if you would only pay attention.

— Can I ask you something?

I don't remind her of the list of questions she waved in my face the day she arrived. I haven't the energy to ask if this is a question that didn't make it onto her top-ten list of things she wants to know. After all this, what's left? I'm curious.

— Yes. What is it? If it's the date of my wedding anniversary, you're too late. That's come and gone without fanfare.

She shakes her head, no, it's not that.

Then perhaps the other, what she's been waiting for all these weeks, walking past the room with the locked door, hand lingering on the white porcelain knob, knowing better than to ask.

No, not that. Instead, she begins to describe a night spent with her father, a starry night when the warm waters of Roanoke Sound glittered with phosphorescence. Her eyes glisten with memory's own lubricant, salt tears, and she moistens her lips, as if she could taste the saltwater.

She tells how each aimless stroke of his oar trailed fire as they floated, adrift. Sparks flew from her fingertips as her hand made figure-eights in the water. A fish jumped, its splash beaded golden, making rings in the water that sparkled in widening circles of light.

She tells me her father cried. Says he told her that he'd once swum with someone else he loved dearly, on a night just like this.

— It was you, Gilly says. His tears were for you. And now after spending these weeks with you, I see why.

Holding onto a chair arm here, a table edge there, I walk to the window where she stands, looking out at the salt roses, brilliant red against the blue backdrop of the harbor. Hard to fathom how each step now comes weighted with conscious thought, lift this leg, move this foot, brace this arm. All the while, traveling alongside is that younger self who never gave a thought to the mechanics of motion, as though the space between thought and action were no wider than the space between flesh and shadow.

When I reach her, she turns to look at me. I take her hand. When she pulls her cool, slim fingers from my own, knobbed and brittle as twigs, I feel my face flush as if she'd slapped it, reddened by her hand so like her father's. But it's only so she can lean down and put her arm around my shoulder.

I stand warmed by her presence, and by the memory I now share with her, of that long-ago night when he was still mine, when she, or someone like her, was our hearts' own longing, a night when he and I floated and spun in the still waters of the bay. There in the black water jeweled with topaz enough for a thousand ringed fingers, he grasped my wrists and swung me in a wide circle, my hair swooning outward, a sheath of gold that continued to shimmer long after he had folded me back in, our limbs leaving their imprint luminous on the dark eddies that pooled and swirled around us. In the shallows we rose up naked, streaming light, two gilded statues blind with our own bedazzlement.

EIGHTY-FIVE

SO WHAT IF TOWNSPEOPLE TO THIS DAY, some who weren't even born until years after he died, still call Captain Gilead Lodge "the man with two families." If that weren't so, there would be no Gilly kneeling on the porch to give Dash a bath. And that, I surprise myself by thinking, would truly be a shame.

Gilly has managed to insert herself in my galley, as I prefer to call my kitchen, poking through the cabinets and drawers, was this my father's fish scaler, can I have it if you don't use it anymore, I bet you haven't scaled a fish in years. In my bedroom as well, where she's seen her mother's wedding invitation tucked in Gil's shaving mirror.

For all I know, she's rummaged through his wardrobe when I wasn't looking, where his life-saving uniforms, his oilcloth gear, his canvas hunting jacket, and his corduroys, their wales worn nearly flat, still hang, moths making new grooves in the cloth.

She wouldn't have found his chamois shirt, unless she's thrust her hand under my pillow. His wool socks, darned by his own hands on a slow day at the station when ships were pinned in place by the doldrums, those she would have had to pull from under the bottom of the covers on his side of the bed.

Now she's busied herself idly scraping dog hair into a soft golden ball. I get up, pass behind her, and make my way down the hall, knowing she'll follow me to the one room she's not entered in all these weeks.

I pull the ribbon at my throat and the brass skeleton key appears, warmed by my breast. I hand her the key and stand back, arms crossed. Of course she's unfazed, simply takes the key from my hand without comment, inserts it in the keyhole, turns the key and the knob at the same time, and pushes against the door, which opens in spite of rusted hinges.

But she surprises me, stands back to let me enter. Or perhaps it's no surprise—the room is dim, furniture draped, shades drawn. What little light seeps in is crosshatched by cobwebs thick enough to trick the eye into seeing the room as a hazy diorama.

This room I never electrified, for no one but me has set foot in it since Gil left. I light two gas lamps, their small flames throwing outsized shadows on the walls. Coiled strips of wallpaper, the glue long gone, tell a more eloquent story than the imprinted patterns, illustrated with nursery rhymes never recited.

I walk over to the double cradle Gil made, ingeniously designed so that one could rock a single cradle, or both. A darkness hangs over the cradles even as I hold the lamp higher.

— I'll be leaving soon, Gilly says.

I say nothing. How to speak into yet another silence looming over me. What is there left to say except Away. You, too, are going away.

The thought occurs to me that I could lock her in, keep her safe, visit her at will.

She walks to the cradles, looks in, looks at me.

EIGHTY-SIX

Her last night here, we spend on the cliff. Above freshly turned earth, the furrowed leaves of the salt roses make no complaint against the wind. One pale pink lobe, the merest blush, detaches from its fringed yellow center. The petal drops, a bead of dew still clinging to its recollection of bud yet unfurled.

All my wars ended, hers yet to begin. This daughter now mine, will I see her again—on this side of land or in the timeless between, it will not matter. Who can measure it, the changing of the tide, the tuck of a bird's wing.

The present is a meticulous place, demanding attention. Can I live here? Who will I be, unburdened by old stories, unfevered by dreams?

I unhinge all my doors, dismantle the walls, pry up the stair treads, pull the panes from their mullions, step up onto the mantel, and leap.

AFTERWORD

ISLANDS, BY THEIR VERY NATURE, impose isolation. Add heat, humidity, and front porches to the mix, and you have an excellent chance of meeting people long dead, who live on in casual conversation and anecdotal asides. Islands are an excellent incubator of stories.

One such story kept surfacing. In fact, it's tracked me my entire life. When I was a child, my uncle introduced me to an eccentric woman who managed an oceanfront hotel in Kill Devil Hills, North Carolina, and like him, I became fascinated with her stories of the Outer Banks. A few decades later, she would become my next-door neighbor. I met her eighty-year-old sister, the woman upon whom the character of Gilly is based, when she moved back to Roanoke Island after an absence of sixty years.

Her father, who inspired Captain Gil Lodge, had been the keeper of a life-saving station, proprietor of three hotels, a renowned hunting guide, a collector of specimen birds, and a contributor to ornithology journals. She was only six when he died at age seventy-five, but her few memories, the swirl of stories surrounding him, and her determined efforts to learn the truth inspired in me a deep fascination. I wasn't sure who intrigued me more: the sisters, their parents, or the first wife he abandoned at Cape Cod.

Initially, I thought the story belonged to the husband, but when the writer Peter Matthiessen told me that often the most powerful narrator of a story is not the one who causes the action, but rather, the one most affected by it, I realized the book belonged to his first wife. I wanted to understand, through fiction, what it must have been like for her to be left, not once, in the most spectacular way possible, but over and over.

I have borrowed from past and present, from the lives of people both met and unmet, from places explored or only imagined. Here are some of the strands, along with a few controversial gaps, which form the historical record.

Why did the man upon whom I've modeled Captain Lodge disappear "between tides," as described in an article written some fifty years after the fact? Why, according to a court transcript, did he take on an assumed name, to be discovered only after his prowess during a life-saving rescue at Chicamacomico proved his true identity?

There were many discrepancies. News stories multiplied, from New Bedford to Barnstable to Yarmouth and back to Chatham. One article said his wife and her niece had made the arduous journey to Hatteras Island to bring him home; meanwhile, another reported that he was returned to Boston, where his wife met him and took him back to Chatham. A story in *The New York Times* said the man had been found "living in the woods in a hut, subsisting on fish and game," and that it was believed "he will probably never be able to perform any mental work again, although his insanity is of a harmless type."

Similarly, I found conflicting information on why and how he left his post as keeper of the Chatham Beach Life-Saving Station and whether, as his hometown newspaper speculated, "there was a woman in it." At the time of his disappearance his future Southern wife was just a girl of twelve.

I was not able to confirm whether the Gil character and his Northern wife had twins who died at birth, as the Southern family believed. It was well known that he longed for a son, so much so that he named his fourth and last daughter after himself.

When I visited the Chatham Historical Society's Atwood House and Museum, the archivist said, "Oh, yes, the man with two families," as he was apparently known. The man's first wife did indeed take in her sister's children after their parents died, and the boy was beloved by hunters staying at the hotel at Chatham Beach.

As for the Northern wife's intimation that the girl and her sisters were illegitimate, a similar accusation was the subject of a court case in the 1930s. When the Southern family's two eldest daughters contested the settlement of an estate in Chatham, the executor argued that the North Carolina divorce did not meet the legal requirement for separation and therefore should not be recognized by Massachusetts. The appellate judge ruled that, improperly or not, the divorce had been granted, therefore the subsequent marriage was legal, and the legitimacy of the children was not at issue. Decades later, the case was cited as a precedent for interstate recognition of same-sex marriages.

I couldn't confirm whether, as his Southern family believed, years prior to his disappearance he had first come to Hatteras Island in search of information about his brother, a Union soldier. Nevertheless, this speculation provided the basis for a narrative about one of the oddest battles of the Civil War. The strangely titled Chicamacomico Races had a serious mission: the destruction of the Cape Hatteras Lighthouse and the capture of two forts on the island, which would give control of the vast network of sounds along the North Carolina coast to the Confederates.

Rescues and shipwrecks described in the novel actually happened, but I have fictionalized various characters' participation. His Southern family mistakenly believed he invented the faking box;

actually, he made a recommendation to the US Life-Saving Service that the whip-line should be left-hand laid and the hawser should be right-hand laid to prevent the two lines from fouling, which was the method employed by Britain's Royal National Lifeboat Institution.

The story of a man who left the Life-Saving Service in disgrace for refusing to go out on a rescue is at the heart of a controversy that was the subject of a number of magazine and newspaper stories but was disputed in the official record. According to the 1886 Annual Report of the US Life-Saving Service, the station crew set out immediately, but owing to distance and difficult conditions, civilians had rescued all hands by the time the surfmen arrived. The 1887 report stated a flare was sighted at the station, but "thick weather prevented the keeper from seeing the vessel." By the time they ventured out, the five-man crew had been rescued and the life-saving crew was left the task of salvaging her cargo of coal in a winter snowstorm. Silver medals were awarded to the nine civilians.

The rescue took place in 1885; the man in the story disappeared in 1893, so surely there were other factors at play. After he and his men had recovered from *la grippe*, an influenza said to cause insanity, he wrote a letter saying that for reasons he would not explain, he had deserted the life-saving station and was leaving the service forever. His superior acknowledged that since his illness nearly two years earlier, he had not been the same. Contemporaneous medical journals in both the US and France documented the virus's effect on the brain.

Other rescues, such as the *Metropolis* in 1878 off Corolla, North Carolina, are accurately depicted, as well as that maritime disaster's impact on the life-saving service.

The rescue of Captain Best's family was fictional, but the idea for Gil to swim to the wreck was based on the 1886 rescue of the *E. S. Newman* by the only all-African-American crew in the US Life-Saving

Service, stationed at Pea Island on the Outer Banks. One hundred years later, the keeper and crew were posthumously awarded Gold Life-Saving Medals.

The episode about the *Merlin*, based on the British tanker *Mirlo*, torpedoed off Hatteras Island in World War I, was indeed one of the most celebrated rescues in the history of the US Coast Guard, garnering the crew high commendation from both sides of the Atlantic. My main character's participation is fictionalized. The keeper, John Allen Midgett, was related to every man in his crew and all were named Midgett but one.

The two women's speculations about future adventures overseas in World War II actually came to pass. The real-life woman who inspired Gilly told me how, after meeting with military officers at a villa in Italy, she was selected as the first female Red Cross volunteer to be sent to the North African front. She was assigned to the 77th Evacuation Hospital working out of tents, which followed just behind the lines so that soldiers could be quickly treated and sent back into battle. During Operation Torch, she suffered a broken leg, which would mean the end of her tour. She insisted, however, that her leg be cast with a metal cleat, as was the British method, so she could to continue to serve. Thirty days after the invasion of Normandy, she landed with the 77th Evac at Utah Beach. She served during the Battle of the Bulge, working out of a schoolhouse in Verviers, Belgium. During her time at Red Cross Headquarters in Paris, she was awarded a Bronze Star for meritorious achievement in ground operations against the enemy in North Africa.

On both Cape Cod and the Outer Banks, the man who inspired Gil was most at home on tidal flats and in the marshes. He held state permits in both locales for the taking of specimen birds, eggs, and nests, and was a contributing writer for a number of ornithology journals. The taxonomic classification of birds has evolved since Linnaeus first designed a system of Latinate scientific names, and DNA research continues to generate changes in classification. I chose to use the terminology current during the late nineteenth century. Given the wide-ranging interests of the man upon whom my character is based, I imagined he would be interested in taxidermy, popular at that time, as was his first wife's art of lace-making called tatting.

Such were the myriad loose threads that, while factually based, gave me permission to depart from history and use my imagination to reweave the story, making it my own. If reading is a kind of retelling, my wish is that this story becomes entwined in your own imagination, so that the tatted veil between writer and reader lifts to reveal yet another story, what you choose to make of it.

—*Angel Khoury*
Roanoke Island, North Carolina

ACKNOWLEDGMENTS

I CAME ACROSS THE UNSOLVED QUESTION at the heart of this story while researching my previous book, *Manteo: A Roanoke Island Town*, at the Outer Banks History Center in Manteo, North Carolina, in 1998. A trip to Chatham, Massachusetts, in 2002 and assistance from Atwood House, Eldredge Public Library, and Woods Hole Oceanographic Institute furthered my interest.

Still, the novel might have gone nowhere if not for the Key West Literary Seminar. In 2008, I happened upon Sterling Webster and his brother, Deems, in Manteo Booksellers. Thanks to Deems's and Liz Lear's encouragement, in 2009 I took my first writing class at KWLS, where Hilma Wolitzer said, "You must finish this." My boundless gratitude goes to workshop teacher and novelist Lee Smith who, in 2015, on the basis of twenty pages, said, "You will be published," and two years later carted the manuscript with her to Italy to see how it all turned out. Novelist Kimberly Elkins, my 2009 KWLS workshop classmate, spent weeks on Roanoke Island in 2017, helping me to round up wayward chapters and sharpen the story's tension. Many thanks to Miles Frieden and Arlo Haskell, former and current executive directors at KWLS, for their encouragement.

Lee Smith led me to novelist Madison Smartt Bell, who as my agent at Ayesha Pande Literary tirelessly championed my work and found its perfect home at Dzanc Books. Editor and publisher Michelle Dotter believed it good, and made it better, with her incisive eye and deeply felt sensibility. I love Dzanc's view of publishing, their passion for bringing books into print, and their incredible and wide-ranging nonprofit support of international workshops, editorial internships, literary prizes, mentorships, residencies, and literacy initiatives in public schools.

All through this long journey—finding the story, and then learning how to tell it—were so many people generous with their time, including my earliest readers, Daniel Khoury, Lena Ann Ellis, Steve Brumfield, John Wilson, Billy Parker, and Terry McDowell; my latest readers, Colby Colasacco, Betty Shotton, Wayne Gray, Nancy Gray, Creecy Richardson, and Sheila Silver; and through all the many drafts, Susan Stewart, aunt, big sister, teacher, friend. For years of conversation and unfailing support, I'm grateful to Betsy Butler, Kat Clay, and Jarie Ebert.

Down through the years, I wish to celebrate my mentors, Francis Meekins, Aycock Brown, and David Stick, who so generously shared their Outer Banks with me. For my first introduction to Cape Cod and Nantucket in 1974, I'll always remember Granger and Dot Frost.

Lastly, I love and honor my grandfather, I. B. Crutchlow, who taught me to look with close attention; my grandmother, Lucile Crutchlow, who taught me to listen for the cadence of story; and my closest family—Lena Ann, Jan, and Buck Ellis, Joyce Trump, and Caitlin Hanbury; my late husband, Daniel; and all my aunts and uncles and cousins—who taught me to believe in "a million tomorrows" on the beaches of the Outer Banks. At the heart of it all is Natalie, who changed my life and infused it with new meaning at a time when I needed it most.